DYING SHEEP

Jesse D'Angelo

Encyclopocalypse Publications
www.encyclopocalypse.com

SPECIAL THANKS

Sean Duregger
John Durgin
Samantha Hawkins
Troy Savoie
Crystal Cook
Stephanie Phelps
Jimmy Turner
My brother, Kevin
And my lovely wife, Lauren
For putting up with me
You rock

CHAPTER 1

Tomorrow I fry.

They're gonna walk me to that chamber, strap me down, and open a curtain so an audience of angry and weepy faces can see. They want to watch me suffer, to hear me beg for my life, to see the fear in my eyes. Ha! Good luck, assholes. I tried to kill myself before, remember? I got no fear of death. Bring on that chair! Bring on the lightning! Never cared about anything before in my whole life, so why should I care now?

I had a good run. I've stalked the streets and lanes and alleyways, terrifying the public. For the past five years, I was the shadow-man, killing indes-indescr... Well, killing anyone and everyone without giving a fuck. Before they caught me, I was a phantom, a faceless beast in the night. Who was I? Where was I? When would I strike again? Oh yes, all the little sheep trembled in fear, and I fucking loved it. After they caught me, I graduated to legend status.

That first news footage of me in cuffs being led into the county courthouse must have scared people shitless. This here country boy was seven feet tall and the outright ugliest sumbitch you ever saw. That's what happens when you put a gun under your chin but only succeed in blowing off your jaw and the front of your face.

It all happened a few years ago. I was thirty years old and dead inside, and one day I just decided to murder

Debbie and the kids because fuck it. Just took out a folding knife and cut them all up in the living room.

I sat in a mess of their blood and guts, feeling nothing. Well, not exactly nothing. I enjoyed it. Couldn't go on like that, had to end it, right? That was my thinking at the time, anyway. Moment of weakness, I guess. So I took the gun, a little .38 I think, put it under my chin. I could barely even get my big finger through the trigger guard, but I managed, and there was a loud *bang* and sparks, and then everything went black.

I woke up in the hospital.

They reconstructed what they could of my jaw and nose, put me on trial, sent me to the loony bin. But I was a good patient, behaved myself and caused no trouble, so when they needed more space for new patients, they let my big white ass go. Or something. Hell, I don't understand how this shit works. All I know is, I was out. I moved out of Chicago, down to Tennessee. Got a job in a factory, went on with my life. But I was no longer dead inside. I had desire now, I had a purpose.

I wanted to kill.

I had enjoyed it and I wanted more. I wondered what it would be like to take down a grown man. To cut a woman's head off. To burn a child alive. There I was, the biggest, ugliest, meanest bastard that ever walked, and I had found my calling. I began to hunt. Targets of opportunity. I had no preferred victim type, no preference about sex or age, mixed up my method of death with each kill. Life was good.

The bodies began to stack up and I became the talk of the town. But I guess when you're seven feet tall, weigh four hundred pounds and your face looks like you got in a fight with a lawnmower, you kind of stand out. So eventually, there was a witness, the pigs tracked me down, blah blah blah. After nearly six years and two hundred and fifty-seven kills, they had caught me.

So now, time's almost up.

My lawyers are done with me and I'm all out of appeals. There's nothing to do but just get it over with and shoot some lightning up my ass. So then who the hell is this coming to visit me? I got no more family, no friends. Maybe it's Detective Brown coming to rub it in, or to get the locations of the bodies they never found.

Either way, I'm annoyed.

The guards tell me to stand and put my hands through the window in the door. They click handcuffs on me, the extra-large size, still barely fitting around my wrists. They lead me out into the hall, the two puny little pigs standing on each side. We head through the block, and I see the other prisoners I pass huddle back into the cells to be as far from me as possible. Haha, that's right, pussies. Be afraid.

We head across the courtyard, and I realize this might be the last time I see the sun. I shuffle forward, my legs chained at the ankles. We head into building B, down another long hall, through the dormitory, into the visitation area. It's a long row of ten booths, a plexiglass partition dividing the chairs on either side. Two inmates are there already, sitting at booths, talking to their visitors using the wall-mounted phones. The guards nudge me forward, take me down to the last booth. They point to the chair for me to sit down. Yes asshole, I know I'm supposed to sit there. Cunt. Fucking gut you alive...

So, I sit.

There is a man on the other side of the plexiglass.

He looks middle aged, though trying to hide it with black dye in his hair and beard. His clothes are casual, his way-too-black hair long and stringy. Several necklaces hang around his neck, his top two shirt buttons open. Rings on his fingers. Expensive eyewear. Fucking hippy. Is he chewing gum?

He picks up his phone. I do the same.

"Hey, man!" The stranger says and waves to me. "Wow! Marvin Brumlow! How you doing?" He waits for an answer. I give nothing. "I'm Jim."

I just sit there staring at him.

"Wow, man!" Jim smiles. "You look great! You're huge! You're ugly! Woo! I definitely like what I'm seeing!" He smacks away at his gum, and I want to punch through that damn glass and pop his head off. Still this is different. He definitely has my attention.

"You gon' pr'poth, *Yim*?" I slur. It's a little hard for people to understand me sometimes, what with a fully reconstructed mouth and all.

Jim laughs, "Haha, I kinda am, actually!"

"Ah'm not 'nto guysth."

"Haha! No no, nothing like that, Marvin. I'm a recruiter. Here to offer you a job."

I stare at him. Whatever he's talking about, he's not joking.

"Look, Yim. Ah'm on desth-row. Ah'm gon' fry t'morra. Fug awf, okay?"

Jim smiles and hold up his hands. "I think you might like what I have to offer."

"Yeah, wha'? You gotta yob fuh me, lil' man? You gon'

bweak me outta' jail, put me in a' CIA o' somefn'? Fug awf."

"Oh, no no. Not gonna break you out of jail. Can't do that. No no, you're gonna fry, no stopping that."

"Okay, hab a nice day," I say and start to stand.

"Don't you want to hear my offer?"

"No."

"It will involve more killing. Lots and lots more killing."

I stop, sit back down, put the phone back up to my ear.

"Staht makin' sense, *Yim*. Mah time's kinna lim'ted."

"Well," Jim says and scoots forward in his chair, whispering now. "You've done a great job, Marvin. Made a name for yourself, created a legend. My employer thinks you'd be perfect and I agree. You'd be free to kill and kill and kill to your heart's content. You'd have extra strength, extra powers, you'd be unkillable. We want to recruit you to become a fully fledged boogeyman for our organization."

"Uh huh. An' uh, who isth yaw employa?"

"Satan. You know, The Devil."

"Uh huh."

"See, you would be perfect for the games. You'd be a superstar! With the right promotion and *me* as your manager? Hoo! You'll be the hottest ticket in Hell."

I laugh. Sure, I'll play along. I like this little guy.

"Thounds gweat. Thign me up."

"I'm serious, Mr. Brumlow. Fortune, fame, fun. We hold multiple events each year, *clashes* we call them. Targets are chosen here on Earth, we send in one of our boogeymen, hunt and kill, baby! People in Hell can watch from the comfort of their own homes, or come to the arena and watch live... It's huge!"

I chuckle. "Tha peopa' in Heww, huh?"

"Hell is no different than here, Marvin. I mean, it's crummier, sure, full of sinners, blah blah blah. But it's kinda like downtown LA, or Detroit. People have jobs, go to the supermarket, watch TV, the usual shit. Some people are in positions of power or authority, or celebrity. If you're a big man in Hell, you can live like a king. And let's face it, you're already going to Hell, am I right? I mean..."

"Mm."

"Right. So you may as well sign on with me, be a big shot in Hell, not just some bum. Am I right or am I right?"

I shrug. "Thure, leth do thith."

"You don't believe me." Jim laughs. "That's fine, that's cool, I get it. Nobody ever believes me at first, and why would they? So I'm just going to assume that you want to do this. That once you cross to the other side, you'll be all in. You'll make a perfect boogeyman."

I snort. "Boodeyma'."

"That's right. The Boogeyman Championships."

I explode into laughter. Spit flies through the gaps in my mouth where I still can't close it right. My sides hurt, I laugh so hard. I say it out loud again just to hear it. "Tha' Boodeyma' Championthipsth!" Ridiculous. I slap my hand on the counter and keep laughing. This is fun. I like this guy.

He shakes his head. "Hey, I didn't come up with the name, dude. That's what it's called, okay?"

I nod, still laughing.

"Look, don't believe me now. That's fine. Just hold up your hand and say 'I'm in.' Then I'll come pick you up on the other side. Then you'll believe me. Okay?"

I nod, still laughing.

"So say it."

I hold up my right hand and sit at attention, clearing my throat. "Yeth suh, I'm in. Priva' Mahvin Bwumlow repo'ting fo' duty, suh!" I chuckle again.

"That'll have to do." Jim shakes his head and stands up. "I gotta go now, Marvin. Don't worry about a thing. Tomorrow when it's all over, I'll come see you. Then the fun can begin. Okay?"

I nod and smile. My face nearly folds in half when I smile, the missing front portion of my jaw, now just soft tissue, bends inward and looks disgusting. Frankenstein's monster ain't got nothing on me. But I kinda like it.

"See you tomorrow, Marvin."

Jim hangs up and looks at me. He smiles and shakes his head, then walks through the exit door. I hang up the phone and stand, filling the entire booth. A guard comes to take me back to my cell. I hum to myself. That was fun. Little something to fight off the boredom, break the monotony. What a weird, crazy little guy. Oh, well. Back to my cell now to await the big moment.

THE PROCEDURE GOES AS PLANNED.

It's December 6th, 1980, 11:00 p.m. I'm led out of my cell, showered and shaved. They shave my face, my head, even my chest and legs and arms. Guess those electrodes have to be nice and secure. They lead me to the room. Four big security fuckers flanking me. They all still look like children standing next to me. There is a curtain. There is the chair.

They make me sit. They strap me down.

They attach electrodes to my head, arms, and legs.

They open the curtain and there is an audience sitting behind a window. I recognize many of the faces. The cops who busted me, family members of those I killed. Not one sympathetic face. Not one friend or loved one or supporter. Good. I don't want no pussy shit. I'm the worst of the worst. Fucking shoot me full of lightning and fry my ass. Send me to Hell! Can't wait to be a big superstar! Haha, right!

A minister steps up and speaks some holy words. I don't listen, couldn't care less. The warden steps up next, telling me that now, by the power vested in him by the state of Tennessee, a ka-jillion fucking volts of electricity shall now be passed through my body until I am dead, God have mercy on my soul, and do I have any last words?

"Justh fuggin' do itsh, cunt."

He nods and steps back. Someone comes behind me and puts a hood over my head. I hear murmuring. It's about to happen. I find myself curious about my own reaction. I mean, this is my moment of death, right? How do I feel…? I definitely have an elevated heart rate, but I don't think it's fear. It's more like an actor about to run out on stage. I truly don't care, and I love myself for it. Bring it on, bitches.

Someone throws the switch.

I convulse.

Heat. Fire. White light. Nothing but pain.

Nothing.

CHAPTER 2

I wake up.

Huh? How am I waking up? I'm dead, right? Did it not work? Are they going to strap me down to that chair again? My eyes flutter open and I stretch. No pain. I'd expect to at least have a headache. Not hungry, don't have to piss... Alrighty then. Guess I'll sit up.

"Hey, man." Jim is sitting next to me, smacking his gum and reading an issue of Fangoria Magazine. He smiles casually and flips to the next page. I'm lying on a large table in a cold, sterile room. Medical equipment. Jars with biohazard labels sit on shelves. Three cooler doors built into a cinderblock wall. I'm in the prison morgue. "How you doing?" Jim asks. He's wearing an obnoxious Hawaiian shirt, and my first thought is to rip it off his back and strangle him with it.

"Unnng... Wha' da fug...?"

"Little weird, right?" Jim tosses his magazine aside and stands up, smiling, chewing his gum. "Ah, you'll be fine."

"Am... Am I...?"

"Dead? Yup!" Jim smiles, delivering the news like a meteorologist announcing a sunny day. "Ready to go to Hell?"

This is going to take a minute to process. I'm wearing a purple hospital gown. I look down at my feet and see a toe tag on my big digit. Shit, this is real. But how? Holy shit! My mind is spinning.

"Come on, bud," Jim slaps me on the shoulder. "Let's get out of here before someone comes back."

"B-Bu'... how?"

"Just slip right through the veil, dude," Jim waves his hand and it's like a see-through curtain appears in front of us. "Parallel dimension, man. That's all Hell is. Heaven too. But we don't go there, of course. Don't worry, I'll explain everything. But right now we gotta go."

"Where ah mah clothesth?"

"Oh, here."

Jim passes me a green plastic bag full of my clothes and possessions. Everything I had on me when I was arrested. I open the bag, and it's a good thing I blew my nose off and can't smell anything, because this shit must stink. Dirty, ripped overalls, filthy undies, a wife-beater turned nearly brown. No shoes or socks? Fuck, oh well.

"Come on, someone will be back soon to bring you into the autopsy room. I think we should be gone before then."

I grunt and hop off the table. My feet hit the cold tile floor. I'm about to start putting my clothes on when I notice Jim just standing there looking at me.

"You gon' wastch me ge' dwess'?"

Jim rolls his eyes and turns around.

"Fine, fine. Is this better? Come on, hurry up."

I put on my old clothes after they've been sitting in that baggie a couple of years. But I don't mind. At the bottom of the bag, I find my wallet, a one dollar bill still inside, along with a family portrait taken a lifetime ago in one of those shopping mall photo studios. Me and the family, dressed up, smiling. You'd never guess that only a few months later, I murdered them all and chopped them into chum. I tuck the dollar bill into my pocket for luck. I look at the photo one last time, then toss it away. I don't know those people.

"Come on, man, come on." Jim is getting antsy, waving me towards the weird curtain floating in the room. I see hazy shapes through it, something on the other side. I take a step forward to study it. "Just walk right on through the veil. It's nothing. Pretty cool, actually."

I start to ask a question but then I hear footsteps. Someone's coming.

"Shit! Come on, hurry!" Jim waves for me to follow him, but I'm curious.

I turn to see the door open and a portly male nurse walks in. He must be the one sent to wheel my dead body into the autopsy room. Oops. He stops dead in his tracks as he sees me towering over him. I see the blood drain from his face and terror in his eyes. He stutters and tries to run. Nope. Not happening, buddy.

I grab him by the back of his blue scrub shirt and throw him face first into the steel wall lined with cooler doors. His nose snaps and a small splat of blood hits the cooler door. Nowhere near enough blood. Must have more. He staggers, dazed, about to drop to his ass, but I step up behind him and grab a fistful of hair at the back of his head and push his face against the cold steel. He squirms and thrashes as I increase the pressure.

I feel his skull start to crack like a hard-boiled egg. His feet kick absently, shit and piss streaming down his legs and dripping on the floor as he loses control of his bodily functions. I mash harder, harder. I lean in, putting my full four hundred pounds into it. His head caves in like a gourd. Blood splatters and streams. Eyeballs burst from their sockets. Chunks of skull and brain spill around his feet and mix with his piss and shit. His body stops moving. I mash even harder, not satisfied until his head is completely flattened.

I let go and the nurse's body collapses at my feet. Ahhh yeah, I needed that. I turn and see Jim standing there watching. Chewing his gum. He shrugs, and the look on his face says, *Hm, not bad*.

"Well, that'll work," Jim says. "Actually, it's perfect. Not only will they find your body missing, they'll also find another victim! Marvin Brumlow strikes again! You'll be even more notorious, the stuff of legend! Oh man, am I gonna make you a star!"

"Now ith yo' turn, lil' man," I say, turning to my new friend. I don't need him telling me what to do. I don't need anyone. I shoot out my blood-stained hand and wrap it around Jim's throat, lifting him easily off the ground. I begin to squeeze.

Instantly, I feel a clamping pressure on my own throat, seizing up my airway. I feel intense pain as my neck cracks and circulation to my brain is cut off. I can't help but release my grip on Jim and let him drop. I stagger back, touching my own throat. The pain has gone. What the hell?

"Come on, man," Jim says rubbing his throat, "is that the way start a relationship with your new manager? I'm your *friend*. I'm the one who's gonna cut you the best deals and have you living like a king. Oh, and if you hurt me, you just hurt yourself. We're linked together. So, just chill. Okay, brosky?"

"Fine," I growl. "Tso wha' now?"

"Now, you follow me down the Yellow Brick road," Jim smiles, smacking his gum and gesturing behind him to the shimmery curtain thing. "Are you ready?"

I grumble. I don't like this, but what choice do I have? Maybe he's right, maybe he'll help me live like a king... In Hell. Wow, this is weird. But fuck it, man. Let's do it.

CHAPTER 3

J im and I step through this veil thing and it's like walking from a nicely air-conditioned room out into a summer day. I find myself in a huge terminal swirling with people. They hurry around to gates where trains arrive and depart, bathrooms, snack stands, information booths. Shit, it's like I've stepped into Grand Central Station.

I follow Jim as he leads me through the main concourse, a big stained glass vaulted ceiling above. Businessmen, hippies, whores, construction workers, vendors, it looks like everyone goes to Hell. I smell hot dogs. Jim stops at a snack stand and buys a pack of gum, offering me some. I shake my head. Nasty.

"Come on, man. Let's get you to your hotel. You can rest for a couple hours, then we'll head off to the arena. There's a big clash tonight. Larry is gonna perform. He's one of our most popular boogeymen." Jim struts and smiles, chewing his gum, dodging around the buzzing commuters.

"Uh huh," I say, taking it all in.

We walk out onto the street, and it's a busy, hustle-bustle metropolis. No lava or hellfire. No dragons, no demons. Just people living their lives. Er, afterlives. There are cars and taxis and buses. There are skyscrapers, a blue sky, clouds, birds. It's a bit too humid, and there are homeless people on the streets, along with scraps of paper and trash here and there. All in all, it feels like Detroit.

Just when I start to feel like this has all been a fucked up dream and I'm just walking around on Earth, some trippy-looking motherfucker walks past. He is not as tall as me, but still big. His skin is black as coal, and his eyes are neon yellow. We make eye contact as we pass, and the moment is gone.

"Who wasth that?" I ask Jim.

He shrugs, "I don't know. Some guy."

"Isth he a... demon? A monsta?"

"Something like that. There are all kinds here. Real mixing pot. Especially here, downtown Malavista. Capital of Hell. You got all walks of life here. Families, criminals, bums, cops, celebrities, schmucks, assholes, everyone. Just like Earth, except here, it's forever. And if you get killed, you just sink down to the next level of Hell. All that fire and brimstone shit? That probably exists. We don't know for sure, because just like dying on Earth, there's no coming back. Let's just say every time you die, you go deeper and deeper into the next level down, so to speak. So you will see boogeymen walking the streets, demons and creatures from other parts of Hell, all that good stuff. We got it all. Even Burger King!"

"Tso ith jus' anotha' wat wace."

"That's right! And we're gonna make you the top rat! You're the next big thing! Literally! Oh man, I can't wait to show you the arena! You're gonna love it!"

AFTER SOME REST and a shower at the hotel, Jim takes me to the arena. There are spotlights outside, flashing neon signs, music blasting, porta-potties. The parking lots are packed, and several groups of people enjoy burgers and beers at their own tailgate parties. Jim is wearing a nice suit and has an all access badge around his neck. He's still chewing gum. I'm wearing the same rags as I came in, still barefoot. Shit, not like I can find shoes my size anyway.

An animated billboard showcases the event, the words "Tonight! Larry is back for blood!" flash on the screen. He's a skinny guy in a gray trench coat, and while his hands look normal, the skin has been flayed from his head, leaving just skull and musculature, and steel jaws with blades for teeth have been screwed onto his own mouth. Pretty creepy looking dude. Still, I bet I'd kick his ass. Larry strikes a few menacing poses, drags his thumb across his throat, tries to look tough. Pfft, whatever.

Jim flashes his badge to the security guard, who lets us in. People here and there are looking at me. Guess I've already made a bit of a name for myself. All those headlines back on Earth, word spreads. Jim is right, I'm a shoe-in to take this game by storm. I'm gonna be king of this bitch. Maybe I can even afford a pair of shoes that fits.

Jim leads me into the stadium to find our seats, slapping hands and giving bro-hugs and introducing me around. I nod and shake hands but don't say anything. Don't much like to talk. I'm just taking it all in. People are all dressed up, having drinks, talking and laughing.

We go to the VIP section where there is a booth reserved for us. I have a perfect view of the huge arena, thousands of seats, all sold out. In the center, instead of a football field or a boxing ring, there is a large stage, eight enormous TV screens positioned in a circle above it. That annoying new song "Celebration" by Kool & The Gang seems to be a hit down here too, and they are blasting that crap through the speakers. Ugh. Security guards surround the stage. Four hot ring girls in bikinis come out, waving to the crowd. The show is starting.

"Tso... How doth thith work?"

"Well, first the commission chooses a target. Sometimes it's a family, sometimes it's a group of teenagers, sometimes it's just one person. The Boogeyman goes through the veil and has twenty-four hours to take them all out. Here in Hell, it's two hours, 'cause time is different here. The hunt is broken up into three periods. When a period is over, you're automatically pulled back through the veil, and you have to stop the hunt for one minute. If you are stabbed, or shot, or run over, or killed, you are pulled back through the veil for another minute. If you are killed three times, that's it, game over. You don't come back after that."

"Too many ru'es."

"Well, it is a game. You don't just go in, kill everyone, and leave. This is entertainment. You have to make it interesting, build some suspense, give the crowd a show. We have to give the targets a chance to win, or escape, otherwise it's not interesting. Oh wait, here we go! It's starting!"

The lights go down. A spotlight shines on the stage, and a portly man in a red tuxedo struts out with a microphone to the sounds of thunderous applause. He spins and plays to the crowd and finally screams, "Helloooooo Hell!!! Are you ready??"

Everyone cheers. He continues.

"Tonight! Live from the Grand Malavista Ampitheatre, the World Champion Boogeyman is back for more blood! The worst of the worst, the monster inside your head, the jaws of death, The Snapper himself, the one and only... Larry Lindner!"

There he is, that bloody red skull with steel jaws and teeth anchored to his mouth, strutting into the arena. He throws up his hands as he makes his way to the stage, and everybody loses their shit. Buzzing in the air around him are what look like eight hummingbirds. I lean in and squint to see better. They seem to be some kind of drone devices the size of baseballs.

"Wha' ah 'dose?" I ask Jim.

"Cameras," he says and blows a big bubble. "They follow the boogeyman around during the clash. That's how we watch the show. They're invisible to anyone on Mid-Earth. See. Look..." Jim points to the huge monitors overhead, each one showing the feed from one of the hummingbird cameras. Hm, pretty cool.

Larry dances and twirls as he gets up onto the stage and is greeted by the red-tux MC Fucker. The crowd is going apeshit.

"Are you ready for bloooooood?" Red-tux MC Fucker screams. The crowd screams back. "Three rounds of carnage, bloodshed, and mayhem! Six unsuspecting high school students in Maplewood, Wisconsin! The parents are gone for the night! They have booze, they have drugs, and they have raging hormones! What could possibly go wrong? It's party tiiiiiiiime!" More screaming from the crowd. Man, they are fucking ravenous. I like it. "Snapper, are you ready?" Larry nods and paces around, hyping himself up. "People of Hell, are you ready?" More screaming.

I lean over to Jim. "Why do 'dey caw him Tsnappa'?"

"You'll see."

What looks like a screen comes down to the stage from the rafters. It's that same shit I walked through with Jim, "the veil" as he calls it. Larry steps up to the veil, rolling his shoulders, stretching his neck, hopping up and down.

"The time... has come... TO KILL!!!"

A bell rings and a giant timer begins to count.

Larry steps through the veil along with the eight hummingbird drones, vanishing from sight. But then up on the screens, there they are. The drones capture multiple angles as they fly around. Wide shots, close-ups, shots of Larry, shots the environment. A few fly away from Larry to get coverage on the poor, unsuspecting victims. I sit back and relax, enjoying the show.

Some hot brunette wakes up, showers, has breakfast with her parents. They leave. She calls her friends. Hot blonde and douchey-Journey fan boyfriend go to the store to buy beer. A cute black couple have sex in bed, then talk about the party later on. Another dude, timid-looking nerdy fucker with shaggy hair and glasses, gets ready for the party, buys flowers. Awww, he must have a crush on the hot brunette.

Jim and I watch their day transpire. Larry watches them. I wonder what the fuck he's waiting for, but I remember Jim saying that's it's all about suspense and entertainment. Not just go in and kill. Larry first likes to fuck with their heads. He appears in mirrors and then disappears. He whispers in their ears and then when they turn around, he's gone.

Night falls. The hot blonde and her douchey

boyfriend get lost driving to the party house. They've been there a hundred times, but they don't realize that Larry has used some super powers to confuse them, sending them down a dark country road. The car gets stuck in the mud. Larry floats in the air above them, menacing them as he finally draws attention to himself. They scream and run.

I lean over to Jim and say, "He ca' fly? Ca' I do 'dat?"

"No. Well, I don't know. Every Boogeyman has different abilities. We kinda have to wait until you get back in there to see what you can do. It might not be anything. You might just be a basic slice-and-dice kind of guy. And that's cool."

"Bu- I wanna hab' powa's!"

"Well, cross your fingers. Oh, here we go!"

The young couple runs into the woods. They are terrified, lost in the dark, confused. Larry uses some kind of magic, because Douchey-Boyfriend-Guy starts to choke and sputter, and his body begins to steam. Hot Blonde cries and asks him what's wrong, and suddenly he howls in pain.

The dude's flesh starts to bubble like water on a stove. Steaming hot blood sputters out of every orifice as his skin melts right off his body. He falls to his knees, gagging and dying, a steaming, bubbling, disgusting mound of goo. The girlfriend screams and cries.

Larry floats above her, cackling an evil laugh.

She squeals and runs into the woods. He appears, then disappears. Appears, then disappears. This guy really knows how to ratchet up the suspense, drawing things out. Finally he grabs her and flies her up into the air, laughing as her dangling feet kick helplessly. He opens up his steels jaws impossibly wide, sticks her head completely into his mouth, then bites it right the fuck off like a grape and blood gushes everywhere. He lets her body drop to the ground, and the crowd around me cheers like crazy.

"Tso thath why 'dey caw him 'Da Tsnappa."

"Mm hm."

The bell rings and apparently the first period is over. Larry steps back through the veil and everyone applauds. Two assistants rush up to greet him on stage, one offering him a bottle of water, the other giving him advice. Once his minute is up, he jumps back in to the clash.

The other four kids begin to party and wonder where their two friends are. They put on Michael Jackson's new "Rock With You" record and dance. The black couple grooves and kisses. The nerdy guy gives the cute brunette flowers, and she's unsure about her feelings. They talk. The black couple moves into the guest bedroom, so the other two go for a walk.

Larry floats right through the walls of the house.

Cool.

He zeroes in on the young couple in bed. He floats into their room and the boyfriend valiantly tries to fight him. He hits Larry with a baseball bat, nothing. Stabs him with a knife, nothing. Larry throws him up to the ceiling, where he sticks, frozen in place. Larry slices the boy's stomach open and pulls out a bloody coil of large intestine as the girl screams helplessly on the bed.

Larry grabs the girl and wraps her boyfriend's intestine around her throat, tying it into a gruesome noose. He heaves her through the window and she slaps against the side of the house, neck snapping like a twig. The crowd cheers.

Then period two is over, and Larry must take another minute break.

When the last two kids come home, there's no sign of the carnage until they get inside. They look around and finally poke their heads into the guest bedroom, where the young black couple are piled onto each other in a mess of blood and guts. They scream and run, but Larry is already there. He grabs the nerdy wannabe-boyfriend by the throat, punches into his chest, and pulls his heart out. He offers the heart to the screaming young girl as a mock present, laughing at her terror.

She picks up the kitchen phone, but the line has been cut. She runs outside, but she is no longer on her suburban street, but in the woods. Larry seems to be really good at fucking with reality. She runs and runs, and finally after Larry has toyed with her enough and put on an entertaining show, he finishes her off with his signature move and bites off her head.

When he's finished, Larry strolls back through the veil and into the arena, holding his hands up to graciously accept the outpouring of love from his fans. I look around to see everyone giving him a standing ovation. Jim included. He's clapping and cheering, chewing his gum.

I sit there and don't move. You can't really tell with my crooked mouth, but I'm smiling. I like this.

I can do this. I'm ready.

CHAPTER

I t's time for my debut.

Jim waits with me backstage along with my "ring men," whatever that means, a doctor, security guards, and president of the promotion, Mr. David Black. The boss man is sharp and fit, wearing a shiny silver suit, rings on his fingers, and diamond earrings. His head is shaved and an amused smirk is permanently fixed on his face.

It's been a week. They've had me in a nice hotel, getting ready. I've signed all my paperwork and have secured myself a three-clash deal. If it goes well and the crowd likes me, I can negotiate for more. I've had meetings with my new legal team and PR people, and I've been binge-watching previous Boogeyman hunts on VHS tapes in preparation. The bloodier and more extreme it is, the more the crowd loves it. Good, I can do that.

I've done press interviews, getting asked the same questions over and over. The people in Hell are pretty amped up to see me in action. While I was alive, I was notorious, infamous. You'd see me on the news after I was caught, but when I killed, it was always in the shadows. Now, it would be for all to see. Would I get shy? Would I have stage fright? Would I get performance anxiety? I don't know, fuck off.

Jim and Mr. Black kept trying to dress me up. They've had their costumer give me different "creepy outfits" and masks to try on. A clown. A blank face. A pumpkin head. Try this weapon, try that weapon. They hand me an axe, a butcher knife, a mace. Yeah, that's all cool, but it just feels too gimmicky. I don't want to be known as the guy who wears this or that mask, or carries a specific weapon.

"It's best if you have an angle, Marvin," Mr. Black insisted. "Some kind of hook. A memorable costume, an iconic weapon. Something uniquely you!"

"Can ah jus' ge' some shoes 'dat fi' me?"

"Haha! You got it. I'll have a custom pair of shoes made just for you. Gonna take a little while, though. In the meantime, is there anything else we can—"

"Nah. Jus' da' shoes."

"So, you just want to wear your overalls and wife beater for your first hunt? Go in barefoot? No mask? No weapon?" Mr. White looked concerned.

I just shrugged. "Yeah, thass' it."

I'm a weapon of opportunity type of guy. Besides, from what I've seen in all these pre-recorded clashes, the audience wants a variety of kills anyway. And a variety of boogeymen. There's Larry "The Snapper," of course, currently leading the polls in popularity. There's a chick they call Bloody Mary, right out of urban legends. There's a guy who can possess dolls and toys, a guy covered in third-degree burns who sets people on fire, a guy who's just a classic werewolf. One chick is called Preying Mantis, and she seduces men, then turns into a fucking mantis monster and eats their heads. She's cool. There's a few guys who are just basic slashers too. Not everyone has some super power or clever gimmick.

I hope I have a super power when I get in there.

Can't wait.

I hear the audience rumbling and clapping. I hear the fat MC-Fucker hyping them up, getting ready to introduce me. I take a deep breath and rock back and forth from my heels to toes. I'm a little nervous, but in a good way.

Jim chews his gum and smiles.

"You're gonna do great," he says. "Just be yourself."

"Mm." Please let me in there already, just to get away from Jim.

I know what I have to do. I've been given a dossier on my primary targets. They are a group of teenage friends celebrating their graduation from high school. One has a rich family who owns a vacation home on a lake in Upstate New York, so they are all meeting up there to party and do what kids do. There's Preston, the rich yuppie asshole whose parents own the house. There's Aaron, the class clown and self-appointed "cool guy." Ross, the dreamy stoner musician. Stuart, the geek who doesn't fit in but somehow got invited.

Then there's the chicks. Samantha is the wholesome girl next door. There's Holly, the track star, brainiac, and overachiever. Then there's Lucinda, and well... Every group of friends needs one slut, right? I can't wait to utterly end their lives in the most painful, theatrical, and gruesome ways possible.

I hear the MC call my name.

Two security guards open the doors in front of me, and I see the walkway stretch out before me into the arena. I glance over at Mr. Black.

"Go get 'em, killer," he snickers.

I nod and begin my walk. I've chosen "Cry for the Bad Man" by Skynyrd as my walk out song. Seems appropriate. The crowd roars and jumps to their feet as I stomp my way in. Those little hummingbird camera-fuckers swoop in around me and follow me up to the stage. I see my beautiful face up on the screens. Lights are in my eyes. The smells of popcorn, hot dogs, and beer.

People on either side of me hold out their hands, so fuck it, I high-five them. Gotta play the part of a celebrity, I guess. I stalk my way up to the stage where the MC—now wearing a gold tux—waves me on. I throw my hands up into the air and turn around for all to see. The crowd is going bonkers.

"People of Hell, are you ready to *rumble??*" The MC Fucker booms.

Everyone screams.

"Marvin, are you ready?" he shouts.

I nod and step up to the veil. I see into the other side, the parallel dimension, the land of the living. Earth.

"Then the time... has come... TO KILL!!!"

The buzzer rings and first period has begun.

I take a deep breath and step forward. I feel my face touch the veil, so soft and fragile, like a ghostly sheet of extra-thin tissue paper. I pass right through it. I feel the air pressure and humidity change as I set foot on the other side. My bare feet step onto wet grass. I find myself standing in the woods surrounding a peaceful, serene lake. The sun is shining. The air is perfectly warm, a pleasant little cool breeze stroking my skin.

Perfect night for a party.

RIGHT. Powers.

Before I do anything else, I need to test out my

powers, or more specifically, to discover what powers I have, if any. Oh, I'll have fucking powers, you know it. I hold out my hands and look at them, start to concentrate. Maybe I can shoot lightning from my fingers, or some sort of tractor beam kind of thing? I point my fingers at a large oak and try to zap it. Nothing. Maybe I can rip the tree out of the group with only the power of my mind, like Luke Skywalker? I strain, trying to use The Force. Nothing.

Hmph. Okay. Well shit, maybe I can fly! I jump into the air, fists overhead, Superman style. I clump right back down to the ground. I try again. Nothing. Maybe I have... Nah. I'm not even gonna try running; no way I have superhuman speed. That would be a cruel joke. Maybe I can transform into some kind of monster? I look at my hands once again, concentrating. Come on, grow some claws! Sprout hair, or scales, or something... Nothing.

Fuck. Come on, man. There's no way I don't have *any* powers. I close my eyes, hoping I have some kind of telepathy, allowing me to read the thoughts of those around me, or to see the future, or... Fuck! I open my eyes and I grunt in frustration. Nothing is working. Shit, even if I do have powers, it's not like I know what they are, and I don't have an instruction manual on how to activate them. Fuck!

I growl and lash out, punching the closest tree.

I hear a wooden creak and a sharp crack, and the whole fucking tree falls over, roots ripping up out of the ground. Whoa! I look at my hands. Look at the tree. The bark is healthy, the leaves are green and vibrant. This isn't some dead, termite-eaten piece of driftwood; it's a strong, healthy tree.

I step up to it, squat down, reach my hands under the trunk. I stand up and lift it all the way to my chest. Whoa! I'm a huge guy, so let's face it, I've always been strong, but man! Lou Ferrigno, eat your heart out!

"Hello?" The voice comes from somewhere to my left. Sounds like either a woman or a young boy. I turn to see a figure approaching through the woods, carrying a small rifle. Young boy. Out shooting squirrels or some shit. Must have heard the tree fall and come to investigate. I stand there, not sure what to do. He hasn't seen me yet. But I see him.

Little thirteen year-old, plaid shirt, that big-bowl haircut that's popular these days. He comes around a row of bushes and finally sees me. Freezes in place. His mouth drops open. I loom over him like one of the trees, not sure what I want to do.

He stutters, staggers, tries to run, trips and falls. Little fucker crashes into ground, right into a knot of roots and small rocks. He squeaks in pain like a little piggy and loses his grip on the rifle. I step over him, contemplating my options. He squirms and panics, turning on his back to look up at me. Finally he screams, tears of terror rolling down his cheeks. I smell urine and confirm the odor by looking down at the boy's crotch. Yup, pissed himself.

He reaches a trembling hand out to grab his rifle. I laugh. Like that little .22 would have any effect on me whatsoever. But I reach down anyway and snatch it away from him. He tries to scramble away, but I gently place my foot down on his chest, holding him down with zero effort. He screams and cries.

Maybe I'll shut him up by sticking the business end of

the rifle down his throat. Maybe I'll just apply a little pressure with my foot and collapse his entire torso, shattering his rib cage and popping all of his entrails and guts like a cockroach.

I see the hummingbird cameras hovering around, looks like three of them are filming right now. Everyone in Hell is watching. No, this kid isn't on the list, but these people want blood. They want guts. They want it extreme. They want me to be the bad man. But they also want suspense and drama, Jim says. Can't just barge in, kill everyone, then walk out. This isn't a race.

This is a show.

I take my foot off the boy's chest.

With almost no force, I snap the little rifle right in half and toss the two pieces aside. The boy scampers back, crawling like a crab away from me. I don't follow. I allow him to bolt away, scurrying off through the woods like the squirrels he was hunting. He'll go home, raving hysterically to his parents, telling them about the giant monster in the woods.

Yes, run. Run, little piggy. Tell your parents, tell your friends, tell the police. There's a big bad man out there, missing half his face. Many won't believe you, but some will. The story will spread. The legend of Marvin Brumlow. The horrible killer whose body vanished from the morgue, and is now somewhere out there on the loose, still killing. Let them be afraid.

Let everyone know I'm back, and I'm coming.

CHAPTER 5

I watch the house from the surrounding woods.

It's a big, two-story number, a luxury log cabin sitting on the edge of the lake. A pier stretches out into the water where a motorboat is docked at the end. A large garage is positioned to the side of the house, its doors wide open. This is where the boat is kept during the winter, along with the waterskis and the family car. There is one car in the donut-shaped driveway, a red 1979 BMW M3. There's one house on the far end of the lake, but it looks like a tiny dot, it's so far away.

Preston and Holly arrived in the sporty little coupe almost an hour ago and I've been watching patiently. I sit and study them, observing through the foliage. Cute little couple. He's handsome and fit, his big fluffy-brown hair bouncing with each step. Little white shorts coming halfway down his thighs and a polo shirt. This is his family's house. Ah yes, the gracious host, unlocking the doors and garage, bringing the boat out to the water.

Holly cheerfully helps him out. Her shorts are even shorter, her blonde hair even bigger and fluffier than his. Her body is toned, tanned, athletic. Little miss track star. She's wearing a tiny little red string bikini top, barely restraining those perky C cups. Mmm, bouncy bouncy, baby. I'm enjoying the show. So are the little hummingbird camera fuckers. Two of them buzz around me while the others follow the oblivious teens. I watch as the little drones circle around the happy couple, getting right up close, but Preston and Holly don't see a thing.

I could just pounce on them, but I'm enjoying the show. Trying to figure out how I should do it, when, and in what order. Gotta build that suspense, Jim says. So I just watch and wait, for now. I can't hear much of what they're saying, but their voices are happy and carefree, and their laughter is annoying. I gather from what they're saying that the others should arrive within the next hour or so. The rest will all be coming together in one car, except for Ross, who's driving up there alone after he gets off work at the Dairy Queen.

With precious little time to themselves, Preston and Holly decide to make the most of it. Well, Preston does, anyway. He comes up behind her as she unloads the last of the bags from the car, squeezing and groping and kissing the side of her neck. She giggles and playfully pushes him away, but he's not having it.

"Stop it."

"*You* stop it."

"Press! The others will be here soon!"

"I know, we have to hurry!"

He wraps his hands over those C-cups. Her head lolls back and her eyes close. He's winning this battle. He reaches down between her legs and squeezes.

"Let's go inside, babe," he says.

She nods and allows him to lead the way, still holding on to each other. They giggle as they stumble up the stairs and slam the front door closed behind them. Time for a better view.

I stand up and stroll along the edge of the woods, closing in on the house. Sneaking nice and slow, I'm careful not to make a sound or be seen as I come out into the open. I creep across the lawn, making my way to the side of the house. The flying cameras follow me and hover as I stop at a window. Inside, Preston and Holly are fooling around, getting hot and heavy. The other cameras float in the air around them, getting up-close angles as the clothes begin to come off.

A proper porn shoot! Cue the cheesy music and send in John Holmes and Ginger Lynn! I watch as Holly's bikini top comes off and Preston gropes those nice perkies! The rest of her clothes come off, and so do his. Skinny, hairless little fucker. Big hair, little dick. Pfft. Can't wait to slaughter this fucking kid. Holly strokes that little dick and gets it hard, and he searches through her big bush until he finds that creamy slit. They fall to the couch, moaning and groaning, kissing and touching.

The cameras watch. I watch. The people in Hell are surely watching, many of them undoubtably jerking off. I could smash in there right now and kill them so easily, but I'm enjoying the show. Suspense! My own dick is getting hard, and I rub it through my overalls. I consider whipping it out right now, but I think I'll save the python for later. Still, I watch as Holly goes down on him, slurping and sucking. After a minute, he spins her around, laying her flat on the couch, and jumps on top. He fucks her. They spin around and she gets on top. She fucks him.

Pretty tame shit for me.

Still, they're enjoying themselves. For these two, this vanilla crap must be super spicy. Enjoy yourselves while you can, kids. He blows his cheese into a condom and they plop down all sweaty and shit, giggling, catching their breath. They decide to take a quick shower before the others arrive, so I go to inspect the grounds a bit more.

I head to the garage and look around. Except for the boat inside, it's pretty empty. There is a box of tools, a generator, a length of rope, a fuse box. I find a hatchet and a box cutter in the toolbox, and now they're mine.

The others arrive shortly.

Preston and Holly run outside to greet them and help bring their bags in. Aaron jumps out of the driver's seat of his Chevy van, a big wave of black hair on his head and a Frank Zappa shirt on his bulging gut. Lucinda in all her blonde sluttyness slips out of the passenger seat, and Stuart and Samantha hop out of the back. Goodie-two-shoes is no supermodel, but she has an earthy cuteness and a big smile that makes me want to cut her head off and turn it into a decorative pillow for my new penthouse in Hell.

Then there's Stuart.

He seems to be the only one here without a date, and I can see why. What a wormy, skinny-flabby, timid, ugly, worthless pile of rat shit. Curly black hair, big nose, pizza face, no self esteem little worm. What is he even doing here? Preston and Holly are an item, as are Aaron and Samantha, and Ross and Lucinda. So who the fuck invited Monkey-Boy here? Oh buddy, I'm gonna have to come up with an extra special, excruciating death for you.

They all laugh and hug and high-five and do all that obnoxious shit that kids do. They haul out their bags, as well as a few cases of beer, and start hauling everything inside. The gang is all here, all except for Ross. Lucinda assures them that her stoner, asshole boyfriend will be arriving soon, and that they should get the party started.

Yes, I agree. Let's get the party started.

THERE'S ONLY one road to the cabin, so that's where I'll wait for Ross.

Perfect time to engage in my new favorite hobby: knocking over trees with my bare hands. I find one on the edge of the road and give it a good hard shove. It creaks and the roots rip out of the ground and the whole thing crashes down across the two-lane road. Try getting past that, hippie.

I go find a good hiding spot to wait.

Before long, I hear the puttering of a small engine and the distant sounds of Rock music. And here it comes, a shitty old VW Bug convertible, a Grateful Dead tune blaring through the speakers. Oh trust me, buddy, you're not gonna be very grateful. The glorified lawn mower slows down and stops before hitting the fallen tree, and out steps young Russ.

I can smell the pot smoke from here. Scruffy brown hair, crop-top shirt, cut-off jeans shorts. Dumb face. He stands there, hands on his hips, looking at the collapsed tree with awe and wonder. Yes, idiot, it's a fallen tree. No, you can't get past it. But please, keep standing there gawking like a dumb, dead fuck.

"Motherfucker!" I hear him say. He throws his hands up and lets them slap back down to his thighs. "Shit... *Shit.*"

I rustle some leaves to get his attention.

He looks over in my direction. "Hello?"

I do it again.

"Hello?" He starts to come over.

Perfect time to use the veil. All I need to do is focus on it, step back... And there we go! I've moved into the parallel dimension. I'm still here in the forest, but everything is misty and gray. Cool! I see Ross approaching me, and it's like I see him through a frosty window. He walks right past me and sees nothing. Ha! Time to fuck with his head.

While he looks around in the woods, I stroll over to his car with my newly acquired hatchet. I step back through the veil, back into the physical world, lean over the open top of the Bug, and swing the blade right into his radio. Sparks pop and fizzle, and Jerry Garcia finally shuts the fuck up.

Ross scrambles back out to the road after hearing the sound of his radio dying. I step back again, out of sight. He looks left and right, creeping toward his car. Fear in his eyes. Good. He looks into his car, sees the hatchet lodged into his radio. Fear turns to terror. I literally see his face drain of color, goosebumps pop up on his arms, cold sweat on his forehead. He slowly looks around, trembling.

"Hello?"

This kid is a fucking genius.

I'd better put an end to this before he starts running down the street back the way he came. Last thing I want to do is have to chase him. So I step out of the veil behind him. He has no idea; I'm just a phantom appearing out of thin air. He backs up, looks around. Nothing. I just stand there, wondering when he'll notice the seven foot-tall presence casting a shadow over him.

"H-Hello...?"

He takes another step back and bumps into something. Me. He tenses up and trembles as he turns around, looking straight ahead into my stomach. His eyes go up, up, up... He sees my pretty face looking right back down at him. He screams like an absolute little bitch and tries to run. I catch him by the back of the neck and lift him into the air with one hand, turning him around to face me, his arms and legs flailing uselessly. He shrieks and howls, and piss runs down his exposed legs. Ew.

I toss him backwards through the air and he lands on the paved road, bones crunching and skin tearing. He cries and squeals, feebly trying to crawl away. I step over him and ponder my options. How should I do this? I look around and see four of the hummingbird cameras hovering. All the fans in Hell are watching, cheering, waiting to see what I'll do. Hmmm.

First thing that comes to mind is to wipe that dumb look off his face, literally. I squat down, grab the hair on the top of his head, and push his face down into the asphalt. He screams and thrashes as I rake his mug back and forth across the rough surface, scraping the flesh off of his cheeks like I was grating cheese. I stand back up and circle him, contemplating my next move as Ross groans and spasms helplessly.

I pick him back up by his neck. Hm. Can't think of anything particularly original to do here. I have that box cutter in my pocket, but nah. Shit, I can't decide. Fuck it, I'll break his arm. *Snap!* He screams. I break his other arm. *Snap!* He cries. I change my grip, lift him up by his left ankle. I get a double grip and give a good twist, feeling the bones of his leg shatter and seeing two of them pop through the flesh. Ross screams and screams and screams. He falls to my feet, quivering. I lift up my big, bare foot and stomp down on his one remaining good leg, pulverizing his femur, then smashing his foot as well, because fuck it, that's why.

I kick him in the ribs and feel them snap. I kick him again and hear a sharp crack as his spine is severed. I look down as he trembles and squirms and cries and bleeds. I could finish him off, but nah, he'll die soon enough. Better that he suffers a bit longer. I pick him up like a bag of trash and toss his mangled body off the road. He smashes into a tree, cracking his head open, before rolling down the embankment to die. I hear the gurgling, raspy breathing begin to fade away.

Alrighty then... That was fun! On to the next!

CHAPTER 6

Back to the house.

The sun is setting. I watch from behind the cover of trees. The lights are on inside, the sounds of talking, laughter, and Billy Squier singing one of his horrible new hits. Okay, first thing's first, gotta cut these dumb fuckers off from the rest of the world. I walk out into the driveway and pull out the box cutter. *Snikt.* One after the other, I slash every one of their cars' tires. The air hisses out, much like the last breaths of poor little Russ.

Now it's time to disable the phone.

I creep around the house, ducking under the windows until I find the main phone cable. One slash and it's done. Oh, so easy. Unless one of them has a two-way radio in there, there's no other earthly way they could call out or signal for help... Unless they set the house on fire to make a big smoke signal? I laugh. Nah, they're trapped, isolated. They could of course run for help, but that's what I want. Separate them, pick 'em off one by one. But no rush.

Now I can just let them sit and stew. I wonder how long it will be until one of them realizes that the last member of their group is running late. Wonder how long it will be until one of them picks up the phone and doesn't hear a dial tone. Or until they go outside and see their tires slashed. Little by little, the fear will grow. But for now, the party is on. I hear the sounds of laughter and shouting, and beer cans popping open.

"To the class of 1980! Wooooo!!" They holler and toast.

I peek through the window and watch them guzzling their beers. Samantha isn't drinking. She looks uncomfortable with the underage drinking, apparently. Aaron tries to get his church-going girlfriend to drink, but she politely declines. Stuart also looks uncomfortable, but being desperate to please and fit in, he sips at his beer and forces a smile. I watch him stealing glances at the other guys' girlfriends. Poor Stuart.

Lucinda drinks and dances to the music, but there's worry on her face. She checks her watch and frowns. Probably wondering what's taking that boyfriend of yours so long, eh honey? Can't wait for Ross to show up, squeeze that little apple-ass of yours, runs his fingers through that long blonde hair, fuck you good and hard in one of Preston's guest bedrooms? Hee-hee, this is fun!

Speaking of Preston, he and Holly are having a grand ole time. They are basically hanging on each other, each with a beer in hand. Yuppie-boy has sparked up a joint and holds the smoke in as he passes it around. It finds its way to Stuart, who just stares at it tentatively.

"It... It won't make me like, see anything funny, right?"

"Stuart, it's fucking weed, dude! Come on!" Preston jokes.

"Yeah, Stuart," Aaron chides him, "Don't you want to be one of the cooooool kids?" He laughs and slaps the nerdy little fucker's shoulder. Everyone laughs.

Come on, Stewie. Succumb to that peer pressure, little buddy.

There we go, now he's doing it. He takes one little puff and his face turns red, coughing violently. They all laugh at him. Well, all except Samantha, who pats him on the back reassuringly. Three of the hummingbird cameras hover in the room with them, and the kids are oblivious to their presence. Love it. Aaron takes the joint away from Stuart and inhales deeply.

"You okay, Stuart?" Samantha asks.

"Y-Yeah," he sputters. "God, that burns!"

Bent over, trying to compose himself, his eyes scan over Sam's hips, her breasts. Ahhhh, I get it. She's the one he really likes. Sure, the other girls are hot, but Samantha is more like him, the good girl, not partaking in drugs or alcohol. Wholesome, pure. And what is she doing with that asshole, Aaron?

Oh, I can imagine the thoughts swimming around in Rodent-Boy's head. Poor, poor Stuart. You won't be stealing Samantha away from Aaron. You won't be scoring tonight, or any other night. You're going to die a virgin, a horrific, gruesome death.

Lucinda checks her watch again, getting more annoyed.

"Where the hell is Ross?" She whines. "He should've been here like an hour ago."

Hee-Heeeeeee.

"He'll be here," Holly assures her. "Don't worry."

No, worry. I watch as Lucinda's dancing fades and finally stops. She looks out the front window. She walks to the front door and goes outside. I creep around the house to get a better look, but I'm not exactly built for stealth. When I peer around the edge of the house, I see Lucinda standing there on the front porch, looking out to the driveway and up the road. She just stands there, rubbing her bare arms.

I could take her out right now. Nah, think I'll wait.

Lucinda turns and skips back into the house.

The others have moved out onto the back porch, dancing and smoking and drinking. I watch them from behind the corner as they pass the joint around. What it must be like to have friends! I scan the scene and notice the kitchen on the opposite end of the house. Nobody's in there. Fuck it.

I sneak around to the front of the house, circling around to the kitchen window. Through the glass I can see bags of food and snacks. A pizza box sits on the counter, along with a bag of popcorn, Corn Nuts, a bucket of Kentucky Fried Chicken, two 2-liter bottles of Coke, and a whole lot of napkins. Mmm, that pizza is calling to me. Should I? I don't think Lucinda locked the door on her way back in... Hee hee.

I reach the front door and twist the knob with ease, then tip-toe into the kitchen. But with a frame like mine, any wooden floor is gonna creak. I stop in place. The distant sounds of the kids on the other side of the house carry through the walls. They can't hear me. I creep in, ducking down to avoid hitting my head, like I'm in a fucking doll house. I reach the island table and loom over the display of goodies like an ugly troll. Pizza box.

I reach and flip open the lid, and look down on the beauty of an extra-large pepperoni pizza. It's obviously intended to be warmed up later, but shit, I'm happy with room temperature pizza. I scoop up two slices and stack them on top of each other. Wonder what these kids are gonna do when they see there's two slices missing? Oh hell, who cares, I'm gonna kill them all anyway.

The double-folded slice goes straight into my crooked mouth and I bite down into all that cheesy goodness. I see one of the hummingbird cameras floating in front of me, getting live footage to show the fans in Hell. I smile as I chew, throwing up my horns Ronny James Dio-style. To all you fans, I salute you. Hopefully you're enjoying the show.

Something catches my eye as I start to leave the kitchen. It's a nice, large, wooden rolling pin. I grab it and take it with me. Hell, I can think of a few cool ways to murder someone with this thing. So, back out the front door I go. I gingerly close the door behind me and run to the shadows.

Chewing is not the easiest thing to do when you have a fully reconstructed mouth, but I make it work. I down those two large slices in three bites. Belch. Oh yeah. I cross around for a view of the back porch, and the group is still partying, oblivious. The new single from Blondie plays on a RCA boom-box, and I've determined one of my kills is going to have to be smashing someone's head through a speaker and killing their shitty music along with them. They all chat and joke around and continue to drink... All except for one.

Where's my boy, Stuart?

I move around the side of the house, looking through the windows. When I reach the living room I stop, seeing the TV flickering inside. Stuart sits in front of the boob-tube, straightening the bunny ears to get a clearer picture. He's watching a news broadcast, with a straight-laced, square-jawed yuppie talking about some bullshit or other. Stuart leans forward and turns the volume knob, and I can now hear what they're talking about... Me!

"The aftershocks of the nightmare continue to be felt. Even after his execution last week in the electric chair, the memory of Marvin Brumlow and his sadistic acts live on," the groomed and polished anchorman speaks in the deepest campfire story-voice he could muster. *"There's still no word from police or authorities from Riverbend Penitentiary on the murder of medical assistant Gary Moore or the theft of Brumlow's body. The investigation is ongoing and police chief Ronald Miner has refused to comment. But how anyone was able to break into the prison morgue, murder a staff member and steal the body of a seven-foot giant remains a complete mystery. Joining us now to explore the psyche of the man who has come to be described as the worst serial killer in modern history, is esteemed lecturer and Harvard criminal psychologist, Doctor Thompson P. Wells. Doctor Wells, welcome."*

This should be interesting. I lean in closer, almost pushing my face against the window, watching the TV screen as the camera pans out and reveals the man sitting across from the news anchor. Dr. Wells doesn't look very impressive to me. Just a middle-aged nerd with a big bowl haircut. He's wearing a brown tweed jacket and a tie that's way too thick and tight around his throat. He seems friendly, intelligent and earnest. Too bad I can't jump into the TV and tear his head off.

"Thanks for having me," Dr. Wells says. Ugh. His wormy little voice makes me want to choke him so hard his eyes pop out of his skull.

"Doctor, what drives a man like Marvin Brumlow to do the things he did?"

"There are several contributing factors that could lead to

the kind of psychosis we see in an individual like Brumlow," Wells continues. *"There are genetics and brain chemistry, for sure, but trauma also plays a big part. In Brumlow's case, there was the physical abuse of his father as well as the emotional neglect and psychological abuse of his mother. His father would beat him on a weekly—sometimes daily—basis, then his mother would blame Marvin for it, and punish him. He was sometimes forced to sleep out in the yard as a small child, or to walk to school barefoot, blaming Marvin for having feet too big to find shoes that would fit."*

Shit, they know about that?

"Then of course, he'd get to school and be laughed at and taunted for coming in barefoot, or wearing filthy clothes, or for simply being so big, and not fitting in. This combination of factors, I believe, formed the perfect storm to create a monster. An individual alienated from his peers, shunned and abused by his parents, knowing nothing but pain and loneliness. It's really no surprise that he would come to derive pleasure from the suffering of others."

Photos fade onto the screen. Pictures of me as a child, as a young adult, smiling with my little family and pretending to be happy. Look at my face, look at that smile. Then of course, they have to show the mugshot of me after my suicide attempt. Gone is that handsome smile. There I am with my nose missing, jagged scars all over my face, my jaw and mouth stitched together with skin grafted from my ass. My eyes look dead and soulless. I don't like looking at myself.

"Dude, what are you watching?" Aaron asks Stuart as he walks into the room.

"It's about that Brumlow guy," Stuart says. "The serial killer."

"Oh, come on, man! Turn this shit off. We're here to party, not look at this sick fucker." Aaron leans over and turns off the TV.

"Hey!" Stuart protests.

"What's up, boys?" Samantha strolls in and drapes herself around Aaron's shoulders. Holly and Preston fall in behind them.

"Stuart and I were just watching a little... Football. Right Stu?" Aaron elbows Stuart in the shoulder, and worm-boy just sighs and says nothing.

"Well, come on, guys," Preston says. "Let's start unpacking the groceries. We'll eat dinner after Lucinda gets back."

Huh?

"Where did Lucinda go?" Stuart asks.

"Oh, she's worried that maybe Ross got lost or something, or his car broke down" Holly says. "Went out for a walk trying to find him. I told her it's a stupid idea. I mean, what's she gonna do?"

"This is Ross," Preston laughed. "Can't get flakier than him. He'll be here soon enough. And she'll be back once she sees how pointless it is. Come on, let's have some pizza!"

Shit, Lucinda left to look for Ross! Perfect! I'd better hurry. Got to be there when she finds his car abandoned on the road with a fucking hatchet sticking out of the radio. This is gonna be good!

CHAPTER 7

Have I mentioned that I don't like running?

Not that I'm actually running right now, but still pushing my big fat ass faster than I like to go. Gotta catch up with little Lucinda. I stalk up the dark country road, huffing and puffing. Guess being immortal and having super strength doesn't also give me good cardio. Dammit. The little cameras flit around and follow me as I plunge deeper into the night.

There's no streetlights around here, just a dark, twisting abyss of asphalt and trees. I don't see or hear anything in the blackness up ahead. Shit, I better pick up the pace. I push harder, go faster... Think I might pass out. But I have to get there before Lucinda finds the car, I have to see her face. I also have to keep her from running away and getting help. And then up ahead, I hear it.

"Ross? Babe?" It's Lucinda's voice.

I hurry around the next corner and finally see her. Those little shorts and bikini top, that long blonde hair. She's holding one of those big, industrial, stainless steel flashlights, the beam good and bright. Looks like I got here just in time for her to see the fallen tree and the VW stuck on the other side. She sweeps the light left to right, not seeing Ross anywhere in the car or the surrounding area.

"*Babe?*" She calls out again.

I creep in closer and watch as she awkwardly climbs over the fallen tree trunk, stumbling onto the other side and crossing to the open driver's door. She shines her light inside and she must be seeing the hatchet lodged in the stereo, because her face drops and her breathing speeds up. She knows this can't be good. Her lip quivers and her eyes fill with tears as she turns around, hands shaking, shining that torch deep into the shadows of the forest.

"Ross! Baby, please!"

Yes, be afraid, bitch. I'm gonna enjoy this.

I come a little closer, then stop, standing still. Then a little closer. Lucinda whips around frantically, shining her light everywhere, looking for anything that might give her answers. She sees the dried blood and ribbons of flesh on the asphalt, the residue of my previous encounter with her boyfriend, Cheech. Any doubt has left her eyes. She knows. Dread has set in. She backs up and staggers around, the beam of the flashlight swinging right into my eyes. She stops.

She sees the seven foot monster standing on the other side of the fallen tree. She sees the hulking beast, filthy and hairy, horribly scarred and inhuman, gripping a large rolling pin. With tears streaming down her cheeks, Lucinda screams uncontrollably. Damn, her mouth opens up wide! Kind of gives me an idea. She turns and trips, running for her life away from me. Shit. I am not about to chase this fucking bitch.

I cock the rolling pin up into the air and launch it hard. It whooshes through the dark and cracks Little Miss Thing right between the shoulder blades. She grunts and falls forward, crashing into the paved road and losing her grip on the flashlight. I see her up ahead, sprawled face-first in the middle of the road, her light beside her, spinning around and casting crazy shadows.

I stroll up to the toppled tree and take my sweet fucking time. I clear the trunk with one step. She's not far away, trying to pull herself up, crawling away. I stalk up to her nice and slow. She sees my filthy, bare feet, and struggles to breathe. Blood trickles from the top of her head down the side of her face. Her palms, elbows and knees are skinned from the impact on the pavement.

"Hewwo Luthinda…" I smile down at her. "Nithe to meeth you."

"N-No," she begs. "P-Please…"

"Look a' tha' pwetty mouf. Mmm… I goth thomthin' big an' harth fo' dat pwetty mouf…" I laugh at her pain as I close in. She is going into shock, fear overriding any survival functions, leaving nothing but a quivering, blubbering mass on the side of the road. Yeah, I got something big and hard for that mouth, baby.

So I take a few steps, bend down, and pick up the flashlight.

It's nice and big and heavy, with a long grip. I go back to Lucinda, who is feebly trying to pull herself away, and put an end to that bullshit. I grab a handful of that fine blonde hair on the top of her head and yank her up to her feet. She screams at the top of her lungs, that big mouth and throat opening nice and wide. Perfect. I spin the flashlight around in my hand, lift it high over my head, and angle her head so that gaping mouth is pointed straight up.

With a hard downward thrust, I drive the butt-end of the flashlight into Lucinda's mouth, shattering several of her teeth. She gags and spasms as the large metal shaft fills up her mouth. I hold her head tight, watching with amusement as she sputters blood and tooth fragments, and I start to apply more pressure to the flashlight.

I hold her head in place, keeping my grip tight on her hair, and shove the butt of the flashlight further and further down her slut throat. I feel it rip past her trachea and into her esophagus, blocking her entire airway. I jam it deeper, and even deeper. I don't stop until all that's left is the light bulb inside of her gaping mouth, still shining bright.

Lucinda's face swells rapidly and turns purple, and a thick cranberry-red foam fizzles from her nostrils as she stares at me with those dumb-fuck whore eyes. I stare right back at her, making sure the last thing she sees in this world is my deformed, evil face smiling at her. Within seconds, I see her fade away, her eyes rolling back and body going limp. I drop the corpse to the ground and step away, pleased with my accomplishment.

The hummingbird cameras take in all the action, and I throw up a little double-bicep pose just to play to the crowd. The fans should love that one. I laugh and look around, suddenly realize that I'm disoriented. Everything is just black and I can't tell which way I'm going. Which way is the car and fallen tree? Hang on a second...

I kneel down and once again pick up Lucinda's corpse by the hair on top of her head, the beam of the flashlight still shining out of her mouth. I angle her head around, using it as a lantern, and there we go. There's the car, the tree. I know where I am now. Thanks, sweetie.

I casually flick her limp body off the side of the road. Who knows, maybe she'll get lucky and land near her douche boyfriend somewhere at the bottom of the dark ravine. That way they can be together!

Now, where was I? Oh yeah, back to work.

CHAPTER 8

I see the lights on inside from a distance as I walk back down that dark road to the house. Pretty soon I hear the sounds of some New Wave Euro pop music shit playing inside. Okay, I'm determined to kill not only these kids, but every single radio and stereo they own. My bare feet crunch down on the leaves and twigs as I circle the house, peeking through the windows.

I see them in the living room, laughing and goofing around. The news has been replaced by Atari, and Preston and Aaron are locked in a heated competition to see who can blow up the other's space ship, or something. Holly sips a beer and cheers Preston on, while Samantha and Stuart sit silently on the couch.

Samantha checks her watch and looks worried. "She's been gone a long time, you guys."

"I'm getting hungry," Stuart says.

"I'm sure they'll be here any minute," Preston says, his mind more in the video game. "If you want, we can throw the pizza in the oven, warm it up. We'll save them a couple slices."

Aaron says, "Works for me. I'm fuckin' starving."

"All right," Preston sighs, pausing the game. "But I'll be back to finish this in a minute. Your ass is mine!"

"Yeah yeah, big words."

They laugh as Preston stands up, stretches, and lopes over into the kitchen. They continue to laugh and talk, until a minute later, when Preston calls out from the other room.

"Dude, what the fuck!" he shouts.

The others head into the kitchen to see what the problem is, and I circle around for a better view. I spy into the window, watching as the five kids surround the island table.

Preston has opened the pizza box, and two big slices are missing.

Oops, did I do that?

"Who ate the pizza, dude?"

"Not me."

"Not me."

"Aaron, got something you'd like to share with us?"

"Fuck you, Press! I didn't take it!"

"Oh, sure. Right."

"I didn't!"

"Maybe Lucinda took some with her..."

"Oh, please."

"Where the hell *is* she, anyway?"

I giggle like a schoolboy, watching my little prank unfold. They continue to argue and bicker, losing their shit over two slices of pizza. Samantha's eyes lock on to something on the floor, and her eyebrows furrow in confusion.

"Guys, what's that?" She points.

They all look down, and though I can't see what's on the floor from this angle, I can take a pretty good guess.

"It looks like a footprint," Stuart says.

"Nah, it's too big to a be a footprint," Preston argues.

"He's right," Samantha points to it. "See, that looks like toes."

"It's just a smear of dirt," Preston says.

"So where did it come from?" Samantha presses.

"I don't know. One of us tracked in some dirt, it smeared, makes it look bigger than it is... I don't know."

Samantha's eyes track around on the floor, and she calls out again. "See? There's another one! And another! Look! They're faint, but they're there!"

"S-So what are you saying?" Holly asks.

Preston shoots a sardonic look at his buddy. "Aaron? Got anything to say?"

"What the fuck, dude!"

"Ha ha, Aaron. Game's over. It's not funny."

"Dude, you think I carry around a pair of rubber Bigfoot feet, get them all dirty and then walk around in here, just to fuck with you guys?"

"Yes!"

"Fuck you, man."

"Where is Lucinda? Where is Ross?!"

More bickering. I hadn't even thought about tracking mud into the house with my big, ugly feet, but it's a nice bonus. Now they're getting worried, afraid. Good.

"Guys..." Stuart's voice trembles. "I-Is there someone else... *in* the house?"

"Oh, shut up, Stuart."

"Baby, are the doors locked?" Holly pulls at Preston's sleeve.

"No, they're not locked. This is the country, babe. There's nobody around for miles. You guys are taking this too far."

"Then who ate the pizza?" Aaron demands.

"You did!"

"And I guess I left the abominable snowman tracks on the floor too."

"That's right!"

"Fuck you, man!"

"Fuck you!"

Holly shakes her head and rushes to the front door, locking and bolting it. The rest of them watch as she makes her way around to the windows, locking them all. "Come on, guys! Are you gonna help or what?"

"Fine, fine..." Preston says, going to help her.

The others follow suit, with Samantha locking the back door, Aaron locking the cellar, and Stuart taking care of the windows upstairs. They all meet back in the kitchen, their nerves spiking.

"You guys happy now?" Preston rolls his eyes.

"I think we should call the police," Samantha says.

"Oh, come on..."

"She's right, babe," Holly urges, "Ross and Lucinda have been gone way too long. Maybe something happened to them!"

"Look, how 'bout I just call Ross's manager at the store? I bet he just had to stay late is all. You assholes just need to relax."

"Fine, good. Call." The look in Holly's eyes tells Preston to take this more seriously. Everyone waits for his answer.

"Fine, okay," Preston says with a sigh. "I'll call the store. Man! This weed is making you guys paranoid..." They all follow Preston into the living room, where a simple rotary phone sits on the counter by the couch. He picks it up, holds it to his ear. Everyone waits. This should be good.

He frowns and hangs up, then picks the receiver up again. He holds it to his ear, clicks the plungers a few times, then gives up.

"Hm. No dial tone."

"What? It's dead?" Holly's voice cracks.

"Shit, dude..."

Everyone murmurs and shares worried looks. Preston remains dismissive as always, waving his hand and trying to calm them down.

"Guys, the line is just down, okay? That's all. Happens all the time up here."

"Preston, this is not normal! Something is going on!" Aaron snaps.

I've had enough of this. Time to take things to the next level.

I turn away from the house and stomp off to the garage. Ducking through the doorway, I head into the dark, open space, heading for the fuse box in the corner. But first, I stop as I'm passing by the tools. A shovel, a rake, a hacksaw, I'm sure there's a hammer and screwdriver in the toolbox, but nah. Instead, I focus in on the gardening hoe. It's old and rusty, a crust of dirt on its edge. Perfect.

I chuckle and step up to the fuse box, throwing open the door. Oh man, I wish I could see their faces when it all goes dark, but I can imagine well enough. I reach up, grab the switch, yank it down. I hear a loud clunk, and all the light coming through the cracks in the walls suddenly dies.

I hear a muffled shriek come from inside the house. Yes! They must be shitting their pants right now. I shuffle back over to the door and poke my head out, looking back at the main house. All lights are off, but I can hear their arguing from inside, the tension in their voices cranked up another notch.

Holly insists there's something going on. Samantha says she's scared. Aaron shouts some curse that I can't quite make out. Preston continues to try and calm them all down. *It's just a blown fuse! But what if somebody's out there? There's nothing to worry about.* Back and forth they go. Preston insists that if there is somebody out there, he'll kick their fucking ass. Ahhh, I love jock assholes.

Mr. Star Quarterback tells them all he's going outside to fix the fuse. I hear Holly remind him of his father's gun, insisting he takes it with him. There's more squabbling inside, and finally after a minute, the front door creaks open. Preston turns on a flashlight and walks out onto the front porch, a gun in his right hand.

I pull back into the garage, closing the door behind me. I creep into the darkest corner I can fit into, waiting patiently. I hear his footsteps coming closer. In a minute, the door creaks open again and there is Preston, shining his flashlight inside. He puts up a facade of bravery, but I can see him trembling.

"H-Hello?"

Why do they all say that? Like the bad man in the shadows is going to answer them! Preston steps inside, swinging his light back and forth. I look at his father's gun, and it appears to be a little .38 snub-nose. How adorable!

I watch as he slowly enters, walking past me and my hiding spot. He shivers, trying to keep the beam of light steady. Inch by inch, he steps toward the fuse box.

"Fucking assholes," he mutters. "Aaron, if this is some

kind of joke, I swear to God..." He moves in closer, closer. I imagine his heart is racing right now. He reaches the fuse box. He swings the door open and shines the light inside.

I step out of my hiding place behind him.

Preston reaches for the switch, but hears my footsteps. He freezes in place. He knows someone is behind him. Trembling, he cranes his head around, slowly turning to look back. The light hits my chest first, then in terror, he points it up, up... Until it finally settles on my crooked mug. Preston opens his mouth to scream, but his larynx seals itself tight. He points the gun ahead, about to shoot me.

I grab his wrist and snap it like a fresh stalk of asparagus, sending the revolver falling to the floor. Yuppie Boy finally finds his voice, and a scream of pure horror and pain erupts from his mouth. Shit, I don't want him alerting the others just yet.

Gotta shut him up.

I step in close, raise the gardening hoe over my head and bring it down in one hard stab. The dull, rusty blade cuts straight into the meat just behind Preston's collar bone. He gags and sputters as I yank the hoe out and toss it away, allowing a spray of blood to gush from the wound. But it's not enough. I stuff my big, dirty fingers down into the wound, getting a good grip on his clavicle and sternum, and give it all a good, hard yank.

His rib cage shatters and rips away from the organs beneath. Tendons pop, flesh tears. One more good pull and his entire rib cage shreds off his body, sending gushing fountains of blood and guts and goo spraying everywhere. Preston's shocked eyes quickly dim, his exposed lungs ceasing to breathe, his exposed heart running out of juice. I watch as it stops beating and his body goes slack.

Yes, die! Die, yuppie-jock-asshole!

I drop Preston's carcass to the floor, his torso torn open, his blood all over me. Good one! I love that I'm strong enough to do that! Let's just see now how long it takes the others to come out and investigate...

CHAPTER 9

The others should be starting to worry right about now.

It's been a couple minutes since Preston left the house to come check on the fuse box in the garage. *What's taking him so long?* they must be wondering. Well, he just got his chest cavity cracked open up like a bag of chips, that's what. I watch the main house through a window in the garage. Nothing yet.

Finally, I see the front door crack open. Aaron, Samantha, and Holly poke their heads out, looking in my direction. They see no light or movement coming from the garage. They mumble and squabble, but I can't hear what they're saying. Finally, Aaron calls out to his friend.

"Preston?" They wait for an answer. Nothing. Aaron is growing impatient. "Yo, Press!" They squabble some more. The girls look especially frightened. Good! Samantha tries to calm Holly's nerves as Aaron takes the initiative to go investigate. He turns on a flashlight—a cheap little yellow plastic one—and grabs a baseball bat. Yes! Maybe I'll shove that bat right up your asshole, hippy!

I back into the shadows.

Preston's body is slumped against the wall where no one will see it until they're right on him. Aaron will come in to look for him, check the fuse box, probably notice that he's standing in a swamp of blood, then finally see his friend. By then, I'll be behind him and it'll be too late. I rub my hands together in anticipation, and wait.

I hear his footsteps, see the weak beam of his flash-light moving between the slats in the walls. He reaches the door. Hesitates. Then I hear the creak of old hinges and the door swings open. With my back pressed against the wall, I can't see him, but I hear him coming, step after slow step.

"Press?" Aaron's voice warbles. "Dude, what the fuck? Where are you?"

Oh, I can feel the kill coming. Hummingbird cameras float around us, just waiting. I imagine the people in Hell are on the edge of their seats, cheering me on. This guy is particularly obnoxious; the class clown who isn't even funny. Everyone wants to see this fucker get dead.

"Press! I swear to God, dude! Come on!"

Aaron is getting closer. Another few steps and he'll be at the fuse box. He walks past me and I stay perfectly still. I hear a squish as he steps into the puddle of Preston's blood. He doesn't seem to notice; must think it's just a muddy spot on the otherwise dry dirt floor. He points the light into the open fuse box, and is just about to begin trying to fix it, when he notices something on the ground.

He looks down, sees red. His light moves across the puddle of blood, finally settling on the mass of flesh crumpled in the dark corner. It seems to take his brain a minute to even process what he's seeing.

"P-Press...?" It's a horrified whisper.

This is my cue. I step out of the darkness and close in.

Then it hits him. *"Press!!"* Aaron begins to hyperventi-late and shake uncontrollably. "Oh my God!! *OH MY*

GOD!!!" Then the dumb shit backs right into me. Thump. I feel his shoulder impact my stomach.

He spins around and before he can even scream, I snatch the baseball bat from his hand and crack him across the head. He drops to the ground, splashing into his friend's blood, a gurgling sound coming from his throat as he bleeds from the new gash across his forehead. He struggles to look up, sees me towering over him.

I grip the bat. Hold it over my head. Gonna bash his cunt brains in, then pull down his pants and shove that Louisville Slugger right up his fucking asshole. He holds out a feeble, trembling hand to defend himself. I laugh and whip the bat down with all my strength —

CLINK.

The head of the bat impacts on a linoleum floor. Huh? What the fuck? I'm not in the garage anymore. I'm onstage at the arena, back in Hell. Fluorescent lights nearly blind me. The crowd cheers from the stands. Security guards, ring officials and other arena staff surround me. Then I hear the smacking and popping of bubble gum, and I know who's standing beside me.

"Hey, man!" Jim beams a bright smile as he chews his Bubblicious. "Great first period! Very nice!"

"Wha' tha fug, Yim?" I'm furious. I look down at his smug face and I want nothing more than to use this baseball bat on it.

"I especially liked that flashlight kill! Very nice, man! Hahaaa, you see, I knew you'd be a natural at this!"

"Yim, I wasth justh abou' to kiw tha' foggin' kid!"

"Ah, it's only for one minute. Look," he points at a

wall clock, "Forty seconds left." Jim slaps my shoulder and smiles.

"Bu' Yim, wha' ith he geth away?"

"That's the name of the game, slugger! Here, have some water," Jim beckons two ring assistants over, two little guys with towels thrown over their shoulders, one carrying a squeeze bottle of water, one carrying a bucket. The one with the bottle holds it up and sprays a stream of water into my mouth. I nearly choke. "Remember, you've got one more period break later on. And if you get killed, you're out for another minute."

I grunt in acceptance. Rules. This part sucks. The little guy with the bucket holds it up for me to spit. Well, I can't spit, so I just let the water dribble out of my hole. Little homie doesn't even flinch as it splashes in there, some of it hitting his face. He's a pro.

Jim slaps my shoulder again, pointing me back towards the veil.

"Okay, three down, four to go," Jim says. "And if that last one gets back to the group, then they'll all know. You'll lose the element of surprise. It'll be harder to pick them off one at a time. Things might have to get messy."

"Thath justh tha way I wike it."

"Okay, ten seconds! You ready?"

I push Jim aside and step up to the veil. I watch the clock tick down. The crowd roars. The buzzer goes off. I don't waste another second, stepping right back into my playground.

I'M BACK in Preston's family's garage. Baseball bat in my hand. Aaron is no longer on the ground in front of me.

Shit. At least Preston's corpse is right where I left it, the revolver beside it. I hear commotion outside and I hurry to the window.

Aaron has made it back to the front porch where the others are waiting. He's a blubbering mess, blood streaming from the head wound inflicted by yours truly. The others seem to be trying to calm him and make sense of what he's saying.

"I-I... So big... He... Preston is... Preston is..."

"Press! *Press!!*" Holly can't contain herself anymore, shouting towards the garage. She starts running down the porch stairs to investigate but the others wisely stop her, holding her back. She cries and struggles, but can't break through. "Preston! Baby, where are you??"

"He's... D-Dead... Someone's here..." Aaron struggles with words as Samantha holds a kitchen towel against his bleeding head. "We gotta... Gotta run..."

"Baby, where are your keys?" Samantha asks Aaron.

"On the... kitchen table..." he grunts.

Samantha hurries inside to get the keys.

"Press!" Holly screams again.

"Can we please slow down here, guys?" Stuart whines, huffing and puffing like a spoiled toddler. "What the hell is going on?"

"Nnng, somebody is here..." Aaron says. "We have to... get out..."

"We can't leave Preston!" Holly cries.

"He's dead!" Aaron urges, holding the bloody towel against his head. "And we... We have to... Ughh..."

Samantha runs back outside, Aaron's car keys in her hand.

"Guys, come on! Let's go!" Samantha shouts. "Come on!"

Goodie Two Shoes helps her boyfriend to his feet, and he still can't balance himself. Holly just stands there crying, and little Stuart takes it upon himself to hold her shoulders and push her onward. The group of four runs down the front porch stairs to the cars. Ah yes, this should be good.

They reach Aaron's van and stop. They notice my handiwork.

"The tires are flat!" Samantha groans. "Look! The back tires too!"

They stand in front of the van, trembling. I can't see their faces from here, but I imagine they're crying, their hearts sinking, finally starting to understand how doomed they really are. But Samantha is stubborn; she runs around the van, pulling Aaron with her, heading for Preston's car. Sorry, honey, I got that one too.

"No!" Samantha shrieks.

Stuart and Holly catch up and stare down at the poor little coupe's slashed tires.

"Oh my God," Stuart whispers. "What do we do?"

"We have to run!"

"Where? We're miles away from anywhere!"

"Well, we can't stay here!"

"Oh, God! This can't be happening!"

I'm getting bored.

Time to introduce myself. With my big, heavy, bare feet, I stomp through the shadows of the garage, pushing the door open. Rusty hinges creak. I step out into the moonlight. The kids slowly turn in my direction.

Their eyes lock on the giant standing across the driveway. They see a hulking beast, covered in dirt and blood, the bottom half of his face a mangled knot of scars. I just stand there. This would be a perfect time for a bolt of lightning, but oh well. These kids are shocked enough. They see me, I see them, and for the first time, we are all on the same page. They know why I'm here.

They scream in horror, and instinct sparks their legs into motion. I watch with amusement as Samantha, Stuart, Holly, and Aaron flee back up to the house, slamming and locking the door behind them.

CHAPTER

Your tires are cut. Your phone is dead. There's not a soul around to help you. What do you do, my little sheep, what do you do?

I stroll around the house, pretty happy with myself, I have to say. I have set the mood for the party ahead. I have shown my face to my future victims, letting them know in no uncertain terms that yes, something really is going on. Someone really is out there. You really are all about to die horrible, painful deaths.

I've created a panic, and it just makes me feel all warm and tingly inside. I smile and kick at pebbles, swing my arms, taking my time and enjoying the night. The cool air, the moon above, the whistle of the crickets. The shocked and terrified sounds of arguing from the four remaining teenie-boppers inside the house.

"It's him, you guys! I'm telling you!" Stuart whines.

"Marvin Brumlow is *dead*, Stuart!" Holly snaps.

"Will you two shut up and help me?" Samantha seems to be taking charge. I hear the sounds of furniture being dragged around, and can only assume that they're barricading the doors with every desk and chest of drawers they can find.

"What are we going to do, you guys?" Holly cries.

"Well, Captain Kirk ain't gonna beam us out, that's for sure," Aaron snorts.

"We have to run for help!" Holly again.

"Go back out there? Are you crazy?" Aaron, I think.

"Well, we can't just stay here!" Sounds like Stuart.

Whatever, I don't care.

I've drifted away from the house, just looking around. I don't need to hear what they're saying inside. They're freaking out, crying, trying to think of a way to escape. Blah blah. I'll let the hummingbird cameras watch them, let the fans see their little drama, feel the tension build. All I have to do is figure out where, when, and how I'm going to make my move.

I could always just smash into the house and hack them all up into little bits. But no, they want suspense, theatrics. So I'll let them sit and simmer for a while. But then what? I don't know, I'm making this shit up as I go.

I pick up a stick and use it like a sword, swatting at leaves, then toss it away. Just snooping around the property to see what I can see. And there is it, the sword in the stone. Or in this case, the rusty old machete in the mud. I reach down and scoop it up, a crust of dirt and leaves clinging to the edge.

Oh yeah, I can murder someone with this.

I need to get them out of the house. But there's four of them, and I can't chase them all. Too young and fast, fuck that. I have to separate them.

I go back to the house and put my ear against the wall. Still arguing.

"You see the house on the other side of the lake?" Holly says. "Look, there's a light on! A little old couple lives there, Susan and Anthony, I think. I met them last year."

"Yeah, so?" Stuart says.

"So, it's not that far! I could run there and use their phone!"

"Oh, come on!"

"What? I'm on a track scholarship! I ran the girl's 400 in 58.5 seconds! I'm the fastest one here, I can do it!"

"We can't risk going out there, Holly," Samantha says. "We just can't."

"That *is* Marvin Brumlow out there!" Stuart throws in. "He's back from the dead!"

"I swear to God, Stuart, if you don't shut the fuck up..." Aaron groans.

It's fun listening to them bicker, but I need to keep this wheel rolling. I have an idea. I circle around to the garage once again and walk in. I look over all the tools, the lawnmower and hedge trimmer, and beside them on the floor, a can of gasoline. Nice. I snag that baby, then head back over to poor little Preston.

I stand over his corpse for a moment and just look at him, admiring my handiwork. He must have a lighter, come on come on, where is it? Ah, here we go, pants pocket. Mine now. I head back outside.

Cool air fills my lungs and I just feel... Happy.

I have truly found myself. This is what I'm meant to be doing. It must be fate. I'm the bad guy. I'm The Boogeyman. And that's fine. I embrace and accept it, no reason to fight or deny it. This is who I am.

I unscrew the lid from the can of gas.

Walking up to the side of the house, I begin to pour the flammable liquid. It spills and dribbles down the side of the house as I walk around structure. I crunch through some leaves as I walk past the living room window, and I hear the kids gasp inside.

"Shh! Did you hear that?" Stuart hisses.

"Oh my God, he's right outside, isn't he?"

Haha, sure am, little girl. I lean in close, pressing my face into the window. I beam that crooked smile of mine and wait for one of them to peek through the curtains. Wait for it, wait for it... Finally, Aaron pulls the curtains aside, and there I am, smiling in at all of them. They scream like nothing I've ever heard and it's fucking delicious.

Aaron whips the curtain closed and I step back, laughing. I hear them all inside, squabbling, crying, their little feathers all ruffled. Poor babies, wait till you see what I do next. I can't whistle anymore, but I can dance, so I dance. I shuffle around and boogie, happy and free. I drum against the side of the house with my bare hands and hoot some unintelligible notes. You like my singing, kids?

Scooping the gas can back up, I continue around the house, splashing it around. I make it all the way around to where I started, then walk out a bit, leaving a little trail. I drop the empty can and take out the lighter. *Flick*, the flame comes alive. I watch the little baby dance at my fingertips for a minute, then toss it into the trail of gas. The fire spreads quickly.

It reaches the house, then rushes left and right.

The little streaks of hot fire slither like snakes, rising up, spreading out. Soon, the house is encircled and the flames are rising. Any second now, my little friends inside will start to notice. Any second... Come on... Come on...

Finally, I hear the wonderful screaming coming from inside, and my soul fills with joy and satisfaction.

CHAPTER

Burn, baby, burn.

Any second now, my four young friends will come running out of the inferno, screaming their asses off. I take a step back into the veil, making myself invisible in the "real" world. Don't want them to know where I am until the last second. Either way, this will be my big finale. I've built up enough suspense, I'd say, given the fans back in Hell what they want. But now I'm tired, my feet are hurting, and I just want to go back to my hotel room and jerk off. Time to wrap this little game up.

I wait outside the back door, assuming they won't be dumb enough to come back out the front. But really, they have multiple options, I guess. Front door, back door, kitchen door, plus however many windows. Shit, maybe I didn't think this through. What if they don't all come out the same way?

And of course, that's exactly what happens. Fuck.

I hear the front door crash open and the sounds of hysterical running. I jog a few feet over to get a better view, and I see Holly hot-footing it towards the road. I'm about to chase after her when the back door flies open, Samantha and Aaron staggering outside. His arm is draped over her shoulder—guess he still has no equilibrium after our little encounter—and they're both coughing from smoke inhalation and struggling to run.

She's holding a large kitchen knife in her free hand, so I guess she gets some points for at least trying to be resourceful.

Shit. The two love birds are closer, but I can't let Holly get away either. And where the hell is Rodent Boy? Shit! Definitely didn't think this through. Still, Samantha and Aaron are much slower targets, so I step back out from behind the veil. I make sure to step on some twigs and dried leaves to ensure a sharp *crunch*, and the cute couple freezes in their tracks.

They turn and see me standing like a monolith.

"Holy shit, run! *Run!!*" Aaron cries.

They run. I follow. Samantha has the cutest little scream, like a terrified bunny rabbit. They stumble and plunge forward into the dark woods, aimless, just running into the night. I march behind them nice and slow, gripping the rusty machete. The flying cameras follow behind me, and some are above. They too are closing in to capture the action to come. Gotta make sure I give them a good show.

Aaron trips and stumbles on the uneven ground. Samantha hysterically pulls at him and he gets back to his feet. She throws his arm over her shoulders again and they hurry into the expansive copse of wilderness, hoping the darkness and trees will hide them, I guess. The ground is uneven, riddled with roots and stones and jagged angles. Branches reach out and stroke them as they run by.

I myself struggle not to trip. Fallen trees criss-cross the landscape, some laying flat, others leaning at different angles. Their massive roots have ripped up out of the ground, their branches broken off into short spikes. The ground rises, then plunges, then swerves left, then slopes down. We are getting deeper into the woods, further into pitch blackness. Fine by me. You ain't going nowhere.

Aaron trips again, and Samantha struggles to help him up. A few feet further along, he trips again. Crying, checking behind her to see me steadily approaching, Samantha strains to pull him to his feet.

"Come on!!" She shouts, forcing him forward.

They're moving again, but Aaron is fading. And I'm gaining.

I may not be fast, but I do have a very long stride. Stomping through the undergrowth, I close the distance. Samantha's eyes look more and more panicked each time she checks behind her. They reach a large fallen tree, cutting in front of the trail at an angle, and choose to crawl under it.

"Baby, come on! He's right behind us!!"

They scrape under the dead tree, its broken branches scratching them as they pass. They make it another few feet before Aaron keels over again. Jesus, dude. Talk about dead fucking weight.

"Aaron, come on!!"

"Sam, run... Just leave me here..."

"No!!"

I'm not squeezing under the fallen tree, so I just step right over it. My toes sink deep into the cold forest mud. Samantha and Aaron turn to face me as I stomp up to them. She snarls and lashes out with her knife, swinging it wildly. The blade slices my forearm and it actually fucking stings. Bitch! I give her a good backhand, sending her flying into the woods. I grab a fistful of Aaron's hair and yank him up to his knees, brandishing my new machete.

Watch this, Samantha. Gonna chop off your little boy-toy's head with one clean slice, then toss it over to you. She screams at the top of her lungs. He just hangs limp, whimpering, resigned to his fate.

I whip the machete down, cutting all the way through his... Oh, wait. Shit. The rusty old blade lodges in the side of his neck and gets stuck. I try to pull it out, but it's jammed in there good. I twist and yank, and finally the blade snaps in two, leaving little bits lodged in Aaron's throat. Thick arterial blood spurts from the uneven wound as Aaron sputters helplessly. Samantha continues to scream. Shut up, bitch, I'll get to you soon enough.

I look down at my poor machete, now just a handle and three inches of decayed steel. Fucking useless. Shit. I toss it to the ground and try to think. Have to finish this douche off nice and quick, get back to the others. Can't let this get out of hand. I turn back to look at the fallen tree. Big, thick trunk, rows of broken branches, now three-foot spikes. Looks like a medieval torture device. Perfect.

I scoop up little Aaron with both hands, hold him over my head, and hurl him at the tree. There is a beauti-ful, juicy crunch as the jagged, wooden stakes rip through fabric, flesh, blood, muscle, sinew, and bone. Three bloody spikes pop through his torso and one through his left thigh, pinning him in place. Aaron gags and chokes on his own blood and bile, his eyes flapping open wide.

Samantha shrieks and cries, watching me turn her boyfriend into shish kabob. She sobs and calls his name again and again, but the light dims quickly in Aaron's eyes. His body goes slack, just dead meat on a spit.

I turn to face her. She weeps, shaking her head, praying to God and begging The Devil for mercy all at once. I step closer. Samantha frantically searches the darkness for the fallen kitchen knife, snatching it up and stabbing it out at me. I laugh as the quivering point of the blade aims at my chest. I step closer.

"Stay back! P-Please... Oh, God!"

She's got spunk, I'll give her that. And thanks for choosing my next weapon for me. Good 'ol carving knife, classic. Maybe I'll use it to skin her alive, then stick her on a spike right next to her sweetheart. Nah, skinning would take too long. I got two other little shits to take care of, and I don't even know where they are. I step closer.

Samantha slashes out at me wildly, backed into a corner, nowhere to run. She begs me to stop, but it's a show of bravado. Her courage is wilting. Her strength is dying. She knows this is it. Any second now, I'm going to destroy her, to violate her flesh, make her suffer and bleed. Whatever dreams and ambitions she has will die right here. Her family will never see her again. Anyone who does see her will likely vomit at the sight of her mutilated, rotting carcass.

Yes, cry and beg, little girl.

She launches a feeble swing with the knife, and I catch her wrist easily. I yank the blade from the poor girl's grip and stand over her, ready to end it. Think I'll rip out her large intestine, tie it around her throat and strangle her with it. Yeah, that sounds good. I kneel down, reaching out to grab her.

"Hey!!" The voice catches me off guard.

I look behind me. No, please tell me that isn't little Stuart pointing Preston's six-shooter at me. He trembles, his eyes intense. Nerd Boy means business. But I laugh. Ain't no way *this* little fucker brings me down. I lurch up to my feet, gripping the knife. I smile my crooked smile and take a step forward.

Boom! Boom! Boom! Boom! Boom! Boom!

The first bullet misses. The others don't. They all hit me center mass, with one piercing my heart and at least two in my lungs. And God damn it, it hurts! I feel the little hollow-points burning into me and expanding in my chest. I stumble back, dropping the knife. My chest is on fire and I can't breathe. I feel a bubbling in my lungs and realize they're filling up with blood.

I feel weak. My limbs are going cold. No!

I fall to my knees, struggling to get back up, but I'm fading. As I collapse onto my back, fighting to draw a breath, I see Stuart run over to Samantha, help her up, and lead her away. No! The last thing I see before everything goes black is the two of them hot-footing it back in the direction of the house.

CHAPTER  12

I begin to steam with fury as I find myself once again onstage back at the arena. The crowd is cheering.

"Easy, Marvin. Come on now, buddy," Jim tries to console me.

"I don' wanna hea' it, Yim!"

I pace around and throw myself a tantrum, the staff wise to keep their distance. Jim stands with his hands in his pockets, chewing his gum, nearly rolling his eyes at me. I grumble and skulk, punching the wall again.

"Remember, you can die three times before you're out of the game."

"I don' wanna die a' aww, Yim! Thisth thsucksth!"

"Stop being such a baby," Jim brings his voice down. "You're doing great. The fans are loving you."

I stop pacing and look at him. "Yeah?"

"Oh, yeah. Look at 'em! The ratings are through the roof. Just chill. Everyone gets shot down or stabbed or crushed once in a while. It's part of the game. Makes it more interesting. Now look, see? Your minute is almost up. That wasn't so bad, was it?"

I look at the wall clock. Eight seconds remain in my imposed break. I shoot a look at Jim and grumble, then take a deep breath and close my eyes. I step back through the veil, feel a change in the temperature, the air pressure, the light.

. . .

MY EYES open to the darkness of the forest.

I'm laying on my back in the dirt, looking up at the stars. I grunt and push myself up, sitting for a moment to catch my bearings. It's quiet and dark, the only light coming from a raging fire in the distance. I feel my chest, looking for bullet holes and finding none. The wounds and pain are all gone. All that remains are my blood-stained clothes.

My hand traces over the dirt, finding the carving knife I dropped earlier. I grip it tight, imagining all the things I'm going to do to little Stuart with it. Time to go. I scoot forward, get up onto one knee, then push myself up onto my feet. Ready to kill. The last thing I remember was seeing Samantha and Stuart running back in the direction of the house, so that's where I'm going.

The flying cameras follow me as I stomp back through the woods, following the light of the fire. Looks like the entire house is engulfed now. My guess is they're going to try and run back down that road they came in on. It's a long way down a dark, winding mountain road, but they could make it. Find a house with the lights on, flag down a car... And where is Holly? I need to pick up the pace.

I pass the burning house and stomp up the road.

I see nothing but darkness, empty and still. Nothing ahead, nothing behind. Shit! Did they even go this way? Did I lose them completely? Damn it! I speed up, nearly running. Within seconds I'm gasping for air, but I push forward. I'm not built for this. I follow the road, going around another curve, then another. I go down a slope, then up a hill, and finally, I hear voices up ahead.

I slow down as I come around another curve, and up

ahead is Ross's car blocked by that tree, and young Stuart and Samantha have found it. I watch as they circle the car, looking for anything that might help them.

"Ross? Lu?" Samantha calls out to the woods.

"Will you stop that!" Stuart hisses.

"Well, what if they're out there and they're hurt?"

"If they're out there, they're *dead*, Sam! Look at this!" Stuart points into the car, and I can only assume he's showing her the hatchet sticking out of the radio. She gasps. "He's been here. We have to go."

I MOVE IN CLOSER, opening up a slit in the veil and stepping in, making myself invisible. I walk across the asphalt, seeing the scene through the veil as I move through the parallel dimension. It's so weird and trippy, I'm there but not there. I creep closer, getting ready to pop out and go buck wild.

"Look, the keys are still in the car!" Stuart says. "Come on!"

"We can't just take Ross's car, Stuart!"

"He's not gonna need it, Sam! He's dead!"

"We don't know that!"

They argue, and I get closer. Closer.

I can't wait to see the look on Stuart's face when I appear out of thin air and start tearing him limb from limb. Only a few feet away. I step over the downed tree trunk, ready to cross out of the veil and flex some muscle.

What's this, headlights? Fuck, of course.

Samantha and Stuart see it too, spinning around as a car heads their way. They gather together to see better as the vehicle approaches. Then their eyes light up with hope and Stuart starts waving his hands over his head.

"Look! Look! It's the police!"

"Oh my God! Help! Heeeelp!!"

Sure enough, it's a black and white patrol car. The red spinners begin to flash and the siren toots as it slows to a halt. Fuck. Samantha and Stuart run to greet the police, and a pair of arms wildly reach out of the back seat, waving at them.

"Hey! Those are my friends! Heeeeey!!" It's Holly.

"Holly! Oh my God!" Samantha gushes.

The cruiser comes to a stop and the back door flies open as Holly jumps outside, running to hug Sam and Stuart. They all fall into each other's arms, hugging and weeping and generally making me want to puke. Two middle-aged, out of shape, mediocre and average in every way cops climb out of their squad car to approach the hysterical group of teenagers.

"You kids alright?" Pig #1 says.

"H-He tried to kill us! I shot him!"

"You shot who?"

"It was Marvin Brumlow!"

"Um, okayyy..."

"I swear, officer! It was him!"

I stand only a few feet away, watching them talk about me. All I have to do is step through the veil. They're all here, all in one spot. But there's two cops here as well, and I don't want to get shot and killed again. Still, I'm here for business. Fuck it. No more of this one at a time shit.

I step through the veil.

Holly shrieks as she sees me materialize right behind Stuart. Before anyone can make a move, my hand is on Stuart's neck, lifting him up, tossing him through the air. He smashes into the driver's door of the squad car, and I hear at least a few bones snap. Don't worry, Stuart, I'm not done with you. I turn to Pig #2 who is in the process of drawing his gun.

Nope, sorry, Pig. Here's a knife in your heart.

I twist the blade deep into the man's chest, then yank it back out, shattering ribs and splattering blood everywhere. He falls down dead. Good enough. Not every one has to be some big production.

Samantha is running. Holly tries to run, but I catch a handful of her hair.

Pig #1 squeezes off two shots, one of them burning into my left thigh. Nope, no way. Can't die again. Must stop him from getting any more shots off. Where's the nearest possible weapon? Well shit, the only thing I have a grip on is Holly's hair. Okay cool, I'll just use *her* as a weapon.

With one good, hard chuck, I send Holly whipping through the air. She crashes into Pig #1 and they fall to the ground. They squirm to get up, both concussed and bloodied from that first impact. I step over them, grab Holly by the ankles, and whip her over my head like she weighs nothing. I bring her down hard, using her face and arms and body to bludgeon the poor cop below her.

After a few strikes—I lose count—Holly is a limp, bloody piece of meat, and so is our porcine friend. I drop her dead body and turn to face my good little buddy.

"Sthuar'… Oh, Sthuar'…" I taunt.

Stuart has pulled himself to his feet, leaning against Ross's car for support. He sees me coming and shakes his head no, silently begging me to stop. Nope, fuck you, Stuart. I grab him and smash his face through backseat window. Shards of glass slice through his face and Stuart cries like a little bitch. I whip him around, smash his face into the rear window of the cruiser.

Stuart falls, bleeding, whimpering, an ugly little shit stain about to be wiped out. I pick him up by his collar, about to deliver some more pain, when I hear a deafening boom, and my rib cage lights up. I feel the burn as a shell of double-ought buck grazes my chest. Somehow Pig #1 is still alive and has managed to grab his pump shotgun from the cruiser. *Chk-chk,* he pumps the action and chambers another round.

He struggles to aim the barrel at me, blinking away the blood running into his eyes. Gotta hand it to the guy, still got some fight in him. But no, can't let you shoot me up. So, still holding onto Stuart's collar, I stomp back over to where the public servant lays squirming in his own blood and broken bones, Holly's shattered corpse sprawled over him. His hand trembles, trying to blow me away.

I stomp down on his wrist, snapping the bones.

Pig #1 wails and weeps. Stuart squirms and sobs, dangling from my grip. I lift my foot good and high, aim, and stop down on the cop's face, smashing his head like an overripe melon. Blood and brains and bone fragments and eyeballs spray all over the fucking place, and a horrified Stuart jerks and screams.

"Oh, God! Oh, Jesus!!"

"Justh you an' me now, Sthuar'..." I laugh, pulling him right up to my face.

"Oh, please, God! Please God, I don't want to die! *I DON'T WANT TO DIE!!!*"

I chuckle as an idea crosses my mind.

Is it too extreme? Ah fuck it, I'm a Boogeyman from

Hell. I can do whatever the fuck I want. So, I bend down and retrieve the cop's pump shotgun. I walk around to the front of the cruiser, Stuart's toes barely touching the ground as I drag him along. He sobs uncontrollably and begs for his life as I toss him onto the hood of the car. I put the shotgun down for a second, then use both hands to yank Stuart's pants down around his ankles. Little nothing dick, as expected. And look at this, baby boy went and shit himself. Nice, a little lube will help.

"Please, I don't wanna die..."

"I know you wan'ed ta' get wucky thith weeken', Sthuar'. Don' worry. I won' wet you die a 'birgin." I flip him around, bend him over, push him face-first into the dented hood of the car. The red lights swirl. The hummingbird cameras wait for it. "No, Sthuar'. Ya' gon' go ou' wifh a bang! Time ta' pop thath chewwy!"

I grab the shotgun.

With Stuart's skinny, bare ass bent over, a slick of shit running from the hole, I take aim. With a good, hard shove, sixteen inches of steel rips up into Stuart's shitter, and he screams so good. Ah man, it's not just a scream, it's a... A bellow. A howl. He is pulling this sound of horror and agony out of his soul, cursing his killer, cursing his maker, cursing the pain. It's beautiful. The excruciating torture, I love it so much!

I pound the barrel in further, and further still.

It tears through his asshole, through his colon and large intestine. I get it all the way in, even the wood fore grip jamming deep into the boy's bleeding shit-hole. I laugh and hoot, enjoying my handiwork as Stuart spasms and shakes like a worm on a hook, an appropriate reaction to being sodomized by a 12 gauge. And no good sodomy is complete without a nice, big, money shot.

I wrap my finger around the trigger. Bye bye, Stewie.

BWOOOOM!!!

The round explodes out of Stuart's chest. His eyes go wide as he looks down to behold the gaping hole and gushing gore. He's fading. Another couple seconds, he'll be gone. Time to put an exclamation point on this.

Chk-chk! I use Stuart's asshole to pump the gun and chamber another round.

I adjust the angle of the barrel, pointing it straight up.

BWOOOOM!!!

Stuart's head blasts into smithereens, little bloody bits of his ugly face flying everywhere like confetti. I take a step back and let his body fall to my feet. A red mist hangs in the air. I could pull the shotgun out of his ass, give Stuart a little dignity, but fuck him. I want him to be found like that.

I take a deep breath and feel good. The fans loved that one for sure. And it's almost over. Just one more little goodie-two-shoes to go.

CHAPTER 13

S amantha has a good head start on me.

She ran back in the direction of the house, so she's either going back to the house, which makes no sense because it's destroyed, or she's going to run around the whole lake to beg neighbors for help, which also makes no sense. I'll get her, but I have to pace myself. The adrenaline is fading out and the pain is coming in.

I have one .38 slug in my leg and a few shotgun pellets in my chest. It burns, hurts to breathe, hurts to take a step. I'm limping, an intense bolt of lightning shooting through my leg every time I put my foot down. Trailing blood. Fuck. I may be super strong, and I may be able to come back after being killed, but I can still *be* killed. And pain is pain, and this sucks.

Limping into the darkness.

I see the house up ahead off the left side of the road. The flames have mostly died down, and the structure is reduced to rubble. Not a whole lot of places to hide, little Sammie. Unless she's really brave, and goes to hide in the hot rubble. Mm. This bitch is starting to piss me off. Why does she have to be so determined to live? She's making me *work* for this shit!

When I was alive and killing, I'd kill one person at a time, maybe two. I didn't go on wild rampages, slicing up everyone I came across. This shit right now is just *nuts*. But it's also my first time, so I shouldn't be too hard on myself. I'll get better. But no, all the more reason to finish what I started, to win this "game," to kill this little bitch.

I make it to the mailbox and begin hobbling down the declining driveway.

The house is charred and in ruins, several fires still burning. It's actually kind of nice. Clear sky, cool breeze, the pleasant crackle and warmth of flames. I kind of want to just sit down and rest... Fuck it. I can rest, can't I? I'm not some machine or juggernaut. I groan as I lower myself down onto a toppled section of wall. Ohhh yeah, that feels nice. I let my head fall back and close my eyes.

I hear a little zooming sound and a whoosh of wind, and open my eyes. One of the little hummingbird fuckers is hovering right over me, looking at me expectantly.

"Wha'?" I hold my hands up. "I'm tathin' a bwea'! Wha'?"

Fucking things won't let me rest. Crowd back in Hell is probably booing me too. In all the hunts I watched on tape and TV, the crowd would always start to boo if they felt things were getting boring. They want nonstop action, the more blood and guts the better. Shit, I hope I've impressed them so far and done enough. But I'm not finished. One more to go, one nice big exclamation point to wrap things up.

I scan the property, looking left and right.

Looks like the cars haven't been touched. No signs of Samantha hiding on the front lawn or around the side. No signs of her on the dock or the trail around the lake. There is still the garage, which is still standing. Yeah, I'll check in there. With a little effort, I force myself up to my feet, then slowly stomp off to do my little investigation.

Might as well look in the cars. I peek inside and don't

see my damsel in distress hiding low and between the seats. What if she's hiding underneath one of the cars? Well shit, I'm not about to get on my hands and knees and get that low to the ground to look under them. I'll just flip the cars over.

I squat down, get a grip, then toss the first car upside down. The second is even easier. No girlie girl, so I move on. I limp around the burning house, enjoying the warmth, and looking behind every shadow and under every collapsed wall. She's got to be somewhere, squeezed into a ball, holding her breath. Hiding in some crevice, throwing lumber and ashes over herself as camouflage.

Keep moving, big boy. I kick over a pile of rubble, look under some collapsed boards and singed insulation, look everywhere I can think of. Next it's the garage, so I hobble over there and throw open the doors. I slowly move inside, and something seems different, but I can't quite place it.

Preston's mangled body is right where I left it. The speed boat is still there on its trailer, ready to be wheeled out to the dock... Wait, that's it! The back doors are open now, and I can see the grass leading out to the lake, moonlight painting the scene on the other side. She's in here, I know it. She's trying to get the boat out to the lake, to use it to get away. Smart cookie.

I creep through the breezy wood frame structure, looking in every nook and niche. I pass the work bench and look under it. Nope, she's not down there. On top of the table is an array of tools, junk and cardboard boxes. There's a toolbox, so I open it up. Looks like somebody's grandpa's tools. These things are old as fuck, but they're in decent shape. I pick out a nice big hammer, good and strong and sturdy. This'll do.

I look under the speed boat, and she's not there. I look inside the speed boat. She's not there either. I move around the front of the boat, slowly starting to check the other side, peeking into the shadows, kicking boxes aside. Nothing. But still, I feel I'm right. She has to be here. I can almost hear her heart racing. She's waiting for me to pass, or find her, and then...? Well, she probably has found some kind of weapon and has it ready, waiting for just the moment to... Oh, shit.

I hear a creak overhead.

I look up. There are big, fat rafters in this place, and Samantha is standing on one of them directly above me. What's that in her hands? Before I can think or act or do anything, she leaps off the rafter, screaming like a valkyrie, lashing down with something long and sharp. It all happens in a fraction of a second.

I feel the impact of four spikes punch right through my chest and knock me back. Samantha rolls off to the side and watches me stagger back, staring down at the pitchfork sticking out of me. Damn it, my heart and lungs are punctured again! I can't breathe and I fall to my back, desperately gasping for air.

Samantha shudders and shivers, slowly circling around me to get back to the boat. No, can't let her get away. I try to move but I feel myself fading. No! Shit, I can't die again, not now! I reach out for her, but she scurries around me. Gotta slow her down, gotta do something.

With my last strength, I lash out with the hammer, bringing it down on her right foot. She shrieks in pain and I feel the bones break beneath her pink Converse. I get a slight satisfaction of watching her stumble and fall, hobbling to get away and crying in pain. But it's short lived. I'm dying.

As my vision starts to fade, I see Samantha reach the motorboat and begin disconnecting the brakes on the trailer. Slowly, the whole rig begins rolling down the hill to the water. No way she'll get away. How will she even get it into the water? How will she... Oh, shit. Everything's going black. Here I go...

Back at the arena. Onstage.

A combination of cheers and jeers from the crowd. Jim does not look happy with me.

"A pitchfork, huh?" He asks.

I grumble in response, pacing. At least the farming tool is out of my chest now and the wounds are healed. At least I can breathe again. But still, this is fucking frustrating. How did this one little bitch get the better of me twice?

My little ringside helpers approach me with towels and a bottle of water, but the scowl I shoot at them does its job, and they scurry away. I growl and look back to find Jim eyeballing me.

"Wha'?"

"Nothing. You okay?"

"Yeth! Justh leab' me awone, Yim!"

Another voice cuts in, and we both look over to see David Black swaggering across the stage to the delight of the crowd, looking dapper as ever in an all-black suit.

"Hey hey! How's it going, you guys?"

"Doing good, Mr. Black," Jim smiles pleasantly.

"Yeah?" Mr. Black slaps me on the shoulder and looks me up and down. "You doing okay, Marvin? Looks like you're having a bit of trouble out there."

"Ah'll be fine," I grunt.

"Good," he continues, "because people are eating this up. Everyone is watching. Everyone wants to see you kill this little trollop."

"Twenty seconds, Marvin," Jim lets me know.

Mr. Black leans in closer and nearly whispers this next bit, "Y'know, there are a lot of people placing some sizable bets on you, big boy. Know what I mean? Don't let us down, okay? If you get killed one more time…"

"Yesth tsir. I know."

"A good beheading is always nice. Crowds love a nice disembowelment…"

"Ten seconds, Marvin."

"Just saying," Mr. Black slaps my shoulder one last time and steps back. He and Jim share a look. The seconds tick away. I step up to the veil, ready to go back in. This little princess is fucking toast.

CHAPTER 14

Back at the lake house, I jolt to life on the dirt floor of the garage. I gasp for air, realizing it's not coming easy. I look down to see the pitchfork still sticking out of my chest. What the... A minute ago I was talking to Jim and it was out and all healed... I guess that's my "spirit form," or whatever, when I'm in Hell, and here in the real world, I'm physical? Right? Fuck it, I got killing to do.

I grab the shaft of the pitchfork and give it a hard yank. Those long barbs squirt out of my torso and I feel immediate relief. The pain has stopped and I can breathe again. I look down at the bloody holes and they have almost instantaneously healed. I toss the fork aside with a grunt, and scoop the hammer back up. Yes, this is the tool I want to inflict my torturous revenge with. Smash up every bone in her body, and then, oh the things I'm gonna do with that *claw*...

Sitting up, I look around to get my bearings.

A chilly breeze blows through the wooden structure. The smell of smoke. The splashing of water... Water! I look out the back door and my heart nearly drops.

Samantha has somehow gotten the speedboat into the water and is just now climbing up into it. Somehow she has the keys, and she's using them. She tries one key after another, but none of them fit. Fuck, I have to move.

I brace myself and haul my fat ass up to my knees. I

plant my right foot. Then I lurch up to both feet. I'm standing. I stretch, pulling my shoulders back, pushing my chest out, feeling my full size and strength. I am charged up, adrenaline pumping, hungry for death. I step into the doorway, looking out onto the lake, and hold my hands out wide.

"Tsamanthaaaa!!"

She stops. She turns. She sees me standing there.

"No... *NO!!!*"

She frantically turns back to the wheel, trying the next key, then the next. I begin to run. There's nothing I hate more, but damn it, she is not getting away. With heavy, stomping feet, I storm out into the night, racing for the water's edge. Samantha screams, shaking uncontrollably, fumbling the keys.

"No! He can't be alive!! It's impossible!!!"

My feet hit the grass. Only a few more steps.

Samantha finds the right key. Twists it. Nothing.

"COME ON!!!" She screams, twisting it again and again.

My feet hit the sand. Hammer up over my head.

She finally brings the engine sputtering to life. Damn it. Maybe I'll get lucky and she won't know how to drive one of these things... Nope. I see her shift gears and turn the wheel, beginning to pull away. Fucking yuppies. I pump my legs harder, splashing into the water after her. My left hand can almost reach the back railing of the boat, but not quite. She hits the gas, picking up speed.

It's now or never.

I jump forward with all my might, reaching out with the hammer's hook. *Clink!* The hook catches on the railing and now I'm being rocketed through the water, hanging on with the hammer while my legs splash behind. The propellor is right next to me, zooming and roaring away. If I slip into it, I'll be even more mangled than I already am. So I keep moving. I pull with both hands until I'm close enough to grab onto the railing.

I drag myself up, peering over the railing to see Samantha up ahead, desperately speeding the boat forward. Out in the distance, there is that one house on the other side of the lake with its lights on. Yes, I'm sure you're hoping you can make it there and call for help. Not gonna happen, honey. I lurch up more, getting a better grip, trying to climb over the railing.

"No! NOOOO!!!" She turns and sees me. She pulls back the throttle and picks up speed, nearly dumping me back into the cold water. But I hang on, pulling myself in up to my waist. Samantha keeps checking behind her, and seeing me coming closer, she abandons her post at the wheel. Hobbling with one broken foot, she snatches up a spare oar, whips it up overhead and lashes it down at me.

The first swing misses, but the next cracks me over the head.

I grunt and fall back, barely keeping my grip. Samantha continues to swing again and again, aiming for my hands. But now the boat is swerving wildly with no one at the wheel, and little Miss Thing is knocked left and right, barely able to keep her balance. I try to climb back up, but she swings again, cracking my left hand. Fuck, that hurts! I lose my grip and fall back, now only hanging on with the hammer.

Samantha turns back to the controls, nearly hyperventilating as she struggles to get the swerving speedboat under control. We are getting closer to the house on the other side of the lake, and as I pull myself back up over the railing, I can now make out it's shape, a two story luxury log cabin with its own dock and boat. Too close.

I have to stop her.

My left hand grips the railing again, and I muscle my way back up. I get my knees on the edge, hoisting myself back in. My waist is up against the railing again, just have to throw my legs over now, and I'll be in. But Sam turns again, sees me, and goes psycho on me once more.

She limp-runs back at me with the heavy wooden oar, swinging it at me as the boat once again goes wild, swerving and bucking like a bull in the water. She lashes out at me with the oar, missing, then again. I swing my leg over the railing and spill into the boat, charging at her. She shrieks and swings at me, but a sudden sharp turn from the driverless boat knocks both of us to the floor.

I get to my knees and start swinging, aiming the steel claws of my hammer for all of her softest, warmest places. My strikes go wild, but one swipe does graze her arm, leaving a bloody slash from shoulder to elbow. She screams in horrible pain. Good, now we're getting somewhere.

She falls back against the wheel, holding her bleeding arm as I slip while trying to get up. She tries to steer the boat, seeing the house and its small dock fast approaching. But here I come again, jumping at her and slashing with the hammer. She jumps aside, rolls away, then ducks the next two swings.

Little things escape her mouth like "help," "oh, please," "oh my God," "please, no," but she doesn't know what she's saying. She is fucking terrified, weeping, soaking wet, in shock. She falls back and I reach for her kicking feet. I try to keep my balance as the boat thrashes around, destination unknown.

She desperately kicks at me, but I catch her foot easily. Oh look, it's the broken foot, what do you know! I squeeze her already broken foot, enjoying the unique howl it illicits from her as I lift her into the air upside down. Time to start breaking some more bones, sweetie. Let's start with this knee right here...

Crack!! I feel Samantha's kneecap shatter and hear the tendons and ligaments pop. I drop her to the floor and watch as she clutches her leg, howling in agony. The boat jerks left, bumps, then yanks right. I keep my footing, closing in as I step over my new girlfriend, watching her squirm beneath me.

"Weady fo' tha' nexth knee, Tsamantha?"

"No, please!!"

I hold the hammer high, about to smash it down.

Then something else smashes. The boat.

We crash into something big, and it does not give. It must be the dock of that house she was aiming for. But I don't have time to think about that now, because I'm flying.

Cold wind, splashing water, weightless. Just flying through the air. I see the dock passing under me. Trees passing on either side, sky above, everything nice and quiet. Until my body connects with the ground, that is. I first collide with the far side of the dock, taking the brunt of the impact on my shins as I double over the side and plummet into the water. Darkness fades in and out.

I hear muffled screaming. Samantha. She's calling for

help. I feel cold darkness all around me. I'm not breath-ing. Must be underwater, possibly floating under the dock, or in the shallows. Either way, there are moments of lucidity before everything goes black again. But I do notice with the last shred of my conscious mind that I'm not breathing. Have to breathe. Have to win. I find a shelf below me, put my feet down, and start pulling myself up.

I hear new voices.

"Oh my God!"

"Sweetie, are you okay?"

It must be the old couple I heard lives in this house. I hear Samantha up on the dock above me somewhere, blubbering and crying. The nice old couple seems to be doing their best to help the frazzled young girl, who is shouting gibberish about some giant man who's trying to kill her.

"P-Please... you have to... he's coming..." Samantha sputters.

"She's hurt bad, Hank," the wife says.

"Hang on, sweetie. I'm gonna tie this around your arm, stop the bleeding."

"Hank, we need to call for an ambulance!"

"We will, Donna. Here, hold this..."

They bicker and do what they can to help the hyster-ical young girl. Meanwhile, I pull myself out of the water and rest against the bank on the other side of the dock. My head is ringing, and I'm struggling to catch my breath. But I look up, and I see all eight hummingbird cameras in the air, hovering around the scene. Waiting on my next move. Can't let my fans down.

I center myself, focus my breathing. The hammer is still in my hand.

"Hank, just go! Call the ambulance! I'll stay here with her!"

"Okay, keep pressure on this! I'll be right back!"

I hear grandpa stand and start running up the dock, back to the house. So I roll back under the dock, get my feet under me, and wait until he's almost made it. And then I explode.

I jump straight up, bursting through the heavy boards and sending splinters and chunks of wood everywhere. The old man screams in shock and terror as I step up through the hole in the dock, all dripping, bleeding, disgusting, four-hundred pounds of me. Everyone screams. The old man staggers back. I lift my hammer.

Chuft!

I punch the pronged claw of the hammer into his forehead, watching his eyeballs fill with blood as his body spasms. Pulling the claw straight back, I rip his skull wide open and let his body collapse into a pathetic pile on the dock, spewing blood and brains, and judging by the odor, also pissing and shitting himself.

"HANK!!!!" the wife sobs.

She is a typical little granny type. Silver hair, wrinkly, spindly, sweet and nice. She must have grandkids and bake cookies, go to church, tend the garden. And judging by that double-barrel on the dock beside her, she also does a bit of hunting.

I step forward, her husbands brains dripping from the end of my hammer. This should be fun. Never did a little old lady before. I stomp closer. The dock shakes. The old lady reaches and grabs the shotgun, and God bless her, she knows how to use it. Before I reach them, she fires off a round, and I feel another cluster of buckshot rip into my guts. I stagger back, grabbing my wound, watching my blood seep through my fingers. No. Not this time.

I lunge forward before she can get off another shot, grabbing the barrel and tossing the scattergun away. It impacts somewhere close by on the beach. I step over the old lady, watching her scream and cry. High-pitched, annoying crying. Yeah, I've had enough of this. I drop the hammer and squat down, wrapping my long fingers all around her head.

I stand back up, lifting her up into the air, her legs kicking helplessly. I look between my fingers and can see one of her eyeballs, panicked, terrified. She knows this is it. I don't have time for anything fancy right now, so I just end her with one good squeeze. Her skulls cracks and pops, and I feel her head give way like an overripe melon. Her eyeballs squirt from their sockets and dribble out from between my fingers, along with her brains, blood, teeth, snot, and that beautiful silver hair.

Samantha shrieks louder than anything I've ever heard as she witnesses the nonchalant way I dispose of her new samaritans. She trembles as I drop the body to the dock, my hand dripping with gooey cranberry sauce. I smile and step forward. She scoots back, back, then with her good leg, launches herself off the dock. I watch her splash into the dark water and begin swimming for the shore.

Okay, sweetie. I'll meet you at the shore.

No way I'm going back into that water, especially not with hot lead in my guts. So I scoop the bloody hammer back up and slowly start strolling back to the shore. Oh man, this would be a perfect time to be able to whistle menacingly. Damn this fucked up mouth of mine! Oh well, I can still hum menacingly, so I do that. Step by step, I make my way down the dock, towards the shore.

I watch Samantha swimming wildly, gasping in pain and choking on water. She makes it to the shallows, crawling on her stomach up onto the shore. What exactly is her plan here? Oh, I see it, the shotgun. It landed in the sand a ways off, to the side. Nope, not gonna happen, honey.

I step over the old man's dead body, then over the massive hole I made in the dock, and finally reach land. I see her crawling away, desperately racing for the double-barrel. Nah, it's too far, she'll never make it. I step off the dock, feeling the grass between my toes.

"Tsamantha... Tsamanthaaaa..." What can I say, I like to taunt.

I close in, gripping the hammer in my right hand. With my left hand, I keep pressure on my wound, trying to keep my guts from spilling out. God damn, it burns like I just downed a shot glass of napalm. I'm losing blood and energy, my strength fading. But I'm almost there. Almost there.

Samantha crawls away, her badly broken leg trailing behind her. She weeps, she claws at the ground, she pulls herself closer to that shotgun. I try to pick up the pace, but my own pain is raging like a furnace. Can't go any faster than I'm going. So I limp forward, almost there. Almost there.

She's almost there too. Another few feet, she'll reach the shotgun. Does she even know how to use it? Shit, from what I've seen of this chick, she probably does. Fuck. I have to speed up, can't let her beat me. I push harder, my guts burning. I grunt and gasp for breath, ready to bring the hammer down on every joint in her body. Ready to jam it deep up into her cunt, twist it around, and use that claw to pull her fucking intestines out.

Almost there. Almost there.

"Tsamanthaaa..."

"*GO AWAY!!!*"

She reaches the gun. I speed up, fighting the pain, almost on her. She pulls the firearm into her grip, scooting around on her butt to face me. Her eyes look up, up, up, all the way up to meet my eyes. I storm at her, hammer raised high.

Her quivering hands turn the shotgun around. She lifts the muzzle, braces the stock into her shoulder. I jump the last few feet, sailing through the air, coming right down at her, hammer swinging...

BOOM!!!

I feel two impacts. The first is a tight pattern of buck-shot tearing through my chest and into my heart. The second is my face colliding into the ground and all the air blasting out of my lungs. I try to breathe but I'm choking on my own blood. And where the hell did she go?

With my last strength, I push up and let myself spin and fall onto my back. To my right, Samantha sits on the ground, muddy, filthy, traumatized, the smoking shotgun in her hands. Son of a bitch... She beat me?

I reach out with my blood-coated hand, trying to touch her, but she winces and pulls back. My hand falls to the ground, splashing into a growing swamp of blood. I can't draw a breath. My arms and legs are getting cold. Blackness creeps in at the edges of my vision. This is it.

Fuck.

Looking at her face in my last moments, I can't quite make out her expression. It's not happiness, for sure. Is it satisfaction? No, she's clearly not satisfied. No, it's a look I haven't seen before, as none of my victims ever survived. It's relief. Just relief in knowing that her nightmare is over. For now. Because if I have my way, I'll be back, little girl. I'll be back.

Right before it all goes black, she hisses "G-Go to Hell."

And it's over. I'm dead.

CHAPTER

Blackness.

Headache. Eyelids fluttering. Lights.

I snap to attention and there I am back onstage at the Malavista Arena, tens of thousands of bloodthirsty fans roaring and cheering all around me. I see my pretty face projected up on a gigantic screen with neon lights flashing, dancing girls, pyrotechnics, the works. The biggest Super Bowl win ever wouldn't come close to this. But I'm confused. Why is everyone so happy and applauding for me? I lost.

The door at stage right opens and out comes David Black, Jim (chewing fucking gum), two bikini girls, and two ring officials. Black approaches me with a smile on his face and a microphone in his left hand, his right hand extended out to me. Okay, I guess I'll shake his hand. This is so weird.

"Marvin, Marvin! Great job in there!" Black says, his voice booming through the speakers. "Tell us, what are your thoughts after your first clash, and how has this experience been for you?"

"Unn..." I hate speaking in public. "I losth, bu' I hab' fun."

"That's all right, buddy," Jim cuts in on his own mic. "You can't win 'em all. But you still did what I knew you would! You kicked ass, you put on a show, you had some really crazy, creative kills, really have your own look and flair! So you did great! Now sure, the purse is bigger if the player takes out every target, but oh well. That's part of the game! And sometimes the crowd likes it when one gets away anyway!"

"There will be more to come for sure," David Black continues, swaggering and making a show for the batshit crowd. "I think Marvin has a lot more hunting ahead of him! Don't you, Marvin?" He holds his hand out to me.

The crowd vibrates the bones of the giant arena.

I smile. I shake his hand.

"Yeth I do."

TO BE CONTINUED...

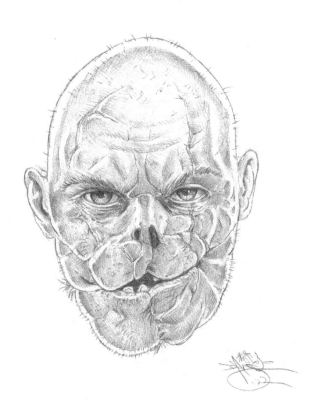

Jesse D'Angelo is an author and an illustrator, born in New York, raised in California, and currently residing in Tennessee with his family. He is a veteran of the film and television industry and has also worked with law enforcement as a sketch artist on multiple criminal investigations.

He writes books, makes pizza and meatballs from scratch, and gets teary-eyed watching cheesy 80's movies.

https://www.jessedangelo.net

ALSO BY THE AUTHOR

Lady of the Lake

Skinner

A Collection of Tails

Prey To God

Doomsday Dogs

Composite